DREAMWORKS

TROLLHUNTERS

TALES OF ARCADIA

FROM GUILLERMO DEL TORO

THE BOOK OF GA-HUEL

Adapted by Richard Ashley Hamilton
Based on characters from DreamWorks Tales of Arcadia series

Simon Spotlight
New York   London   Toronto   Sydney   New Delhi

SIMON SPOTLIGHT
An imprint of Simon & Schuster Children's Publishing Division
1230 Avenue of the Americas, New York, New York 10020
This Simon Spotlight hardcover edition June 2018
DreamWorks Trollhunters © 2018 DreamWorks Animation L.L.C. All Rights Reserved. All rights reserved, including the right of reproduction in whole or in part in any form. SIMON SPOTLIGHT and colophon are registered trademarks of Simon & Schuster, Inc. For information about special discounts for bulk purchases, please contact Simon & Schuster Special Sales at 1-866-506-1949 or business@simonandschuster.com.
Designed by Nick Sciacca
Manufactured in the United States of America 0518 FFG
10 9 8 7 6 5 4 3 2 1
ISBN 978-1-5344-1714-4 (hc)
ISBN 978-1-5344-1713-7 (pbk)
ISBN 978-1-5344-1715-1 (eBook)

EYES OF STONE

Foolish fleshbags.

The angry words popped into Spar the Spiteful's mind as he charged through the humans' pathetic excuse for a city. The Trollhunter never much cared for the hornless, helpless creatures Merlin had entrusted him to defend. And this new village of theirs—this "Sumer," as they called it—paled woefully in comparison to the jeweled majesty of his own underground home, Glastonbury Tor Trollmarket. At least the Sumerians were asleep at this late hour and not around to bother Spar.

This desert heat wasn't doing much to improve his mood, though. Being a Garden Troll, Spar wasn't fond of Sumer's arid winds and sandy dunes. The lack of moisture made his moss itch and his branch-horns ache. Sweating profusely under his Daylight Armor, Spar raced up one of the city's torchlit staircases and jumped onto a nearby house. Amazingly, the roof did not collapse under the weight of the stocky Trollhunter's ironclad body.

Spar vaulted over the wide gap between houses and landed on the next roof. His footing was off this time, causing the Trollhunter to stumble and nearly fall over the side. But he quickly regained his balance and continued running. Spar the Spiteful never broke his stride, never slowed down. He couldn't. Not with a Gumm-Gumm on the loose.

The Trollhunter's keen eyes caught sight of his enemy dead ahead. The hulking, horned monster bounded from rooftop to rooftop, his hooves clattering against the shingles.

"Gunmar the Black!" Spar called out. "Cease your cowardly escape! Come face me—Troll to Troll—instead of hiding behind innocent humans!"

"But I hunger, Trollhunter!" taunted Gunmar, his veins pulsing with pale blue light. "And fleshlings make the tastiest of midnight snacks!"

Gunmar sank his claws into the side of the next building and slid down to the street level, leaving eight deep gashes along the wall in his wake. Spar gritted his tusklike teeth as Gunmar hurried toward Sumer's ziggurat—a squat pyramid at the city's center.

The Trollhunter somersaulted off his current roof and aimed toward a nearby wall. Landing feetfirst on the wall, Spar immediately pushed off again with his muscular legs, carrying him to a second wall. He kept springing back and forth between the two walls, getting lower and lower each time, until he reached the street and took off after Gunmar.

As soon as the Trollhunter entered the ziggurat, he understood that it was a holy place to the Sumerians. Low flames flickered from bronze braziers. Polished metal objects lined the altars. And petroglyphs—crude drawings carved into the sandstone walls by human hands—stretched as far as Spar's eyes could see. He figured the pyramid held thousands of Sumerians during their worship hours. But at night, the deserted temple seemed as silent and lonely as a graveyard.

A scraping noise caught Spar's attention, and he saw something shift in the darkness. The Trollhunter held out his hands and conjured the

Daylight Club. Spar aimed his blunt, silvery weapon toward the temple's shadowed corner. The Amulet on his chest glowed brighter.

"You're trapped in here, Gunmar," said Spar, inching closer. "I stand between you and the only exit. Stop running and face Merlin's justice once and for—"

The Trollhunter reached the darkened corner, only to find it empty. He turned around to see if Gunmar had somehow slipped past him. Looking back, Spar noticed a new detail illuminated by the Amulet. Eight matching scratches ran across one of the large floor tiles.

"Claw marks," muttered Spar.

Kneeling, the Trollhunter pried open the tile with the handle of his club. His Amulet now cast its glow upon a hidden tunnel beneath the temple floor. The passageway appeared far older than the pyramid that sat atop it. Cobwebs clogged the tunnel, and eons of dust coated its floor—except where Gumm-Gumm footprints appeared next to those of another, smaller Troll. Spar wondered if the humans even knew of these catacombs that existed under their ziggurat. Then, a much more troubling question came to the Trollhunter's mind: *What if Gunmar isn't running from me? What if he's running* toward *something?*

The Amulet lit the tunnels like a torch. Spar crept down the passage, sweeping aside thick sheets of webs and keeping his Daylight Club at the ready. At least it felt cooler to the Garden Troll down here. He tracked the two sets of fresh footprints into an underground chamber. Crystals cropped out of the ceiling and floor, lending a dim glow to the cavern.

Spar discovered that the walls down here had been adorned with petroglyphs too. Only these images appeared far more sophisticated than the ones in the Sumerian pyramid, as if carved by a skilled artisan. What's more, these engravings depicted events that no human could—or should— have ever witnessed. Spar's eyes went to one petroglyph in particular, etched in the shape of a bearded man holding a crystal staff. It looked like a wizard. It looked like . . .

"Merlin?" said Spar, his voice barely above a whisper.

Staring farther down the wall, he spotted an

engraving of a puny human boy wearing the armor of the Trollhunter and muttered, "Impossible."

Spar's mind reeled in confusion. He braced himself against the wall, looked up—and saw his own tusked face staring back at him. The Trollhunter pulled away from the wall as if it were white-hot, but his eyes had not deceived him. Spar the Spiteful stared at a petroglyph of Spar the Spiteful staring at a petroglyph of Spar the Spiteful and so on. A dizzying sensation overcame him, as if he were still bouncing endlessly between those two city walls.

"How . . . how can this be?" he asked in confusion.

"Shh!" whispered a new voice.

Spar spun around and found a Troll sitting on the cave floor, scribbling something into a big, heavy book on his lap. Short and potbellied with piglike features, the Troll wore thick crystal spectacles. He didn't even bother looking up as he added, "I'm trying to concentrate."

Disoriented, Spar glanced at the Troll's tiny feet—a perfect match to the other set of prints in the dusty tunnels. The Trollhunter noticed how the studious little creature kept looking back and forth between the petroglyphs and his book as he wrote.

"You . . . you are copying what these ancient walls show," said Spar. "But how can they possibly show events that have just happened—events that have not yet come to pass?"

"You'd have to ask their author," answered the Troll, nodding to the carved likeness of the wizard. "He's left them in countless caves across the surface world."

"Then . . . then this must be the reason Gunmar came here," reasoned Spar.

The crystal pen immediately stopped scratching against the parchment. Leaping to his feet so fast he almost lost his glasses, the paunchy Troll cried, "The Skullcrusher is *here*?! You must protect me, Trollhunter! You must help me escape!"

The porcine Troll scurried behind Spar's armored body for protection. Spar ignored the Troll's whimpers and concentrated on searching their surroundings. But the Trollhunter's always reliable eyesight failed him. Between the faint gemlight and the endless engravings on the walls, he felt overwhelmed, vulnerable.

"The book!" exclaimed Spar. "Its pages may reveal Gunmar's location!"

7

"No!" yelled the Troll as Spar snatched the book from his grasp. *"The Book of Ga-Huel* isn't meant to be read by ordinary eyes! The enchantments used to write it are beyond powerful! If you look upon the latest page before the ink has dried—"

So great was Spar's spite in this moment that he refused to heed the warnings. He flipped to a blank page, which erupted with brilliant, otherworldly light. The glare struck Spar directly in his eyes. He cried out in pain and dropped the book.

"I—I can't see!" Spar cried.

He fumbled his fingers over his eyes, which had turned to stone. The Troll in the crystal spectacles reclaimed *The Book of Ga-Huel* and looked up in time to see Gunmar emerge from the cavern's shadows.

"You always were the better fighter, Trollhunter," Spar heard Gunmar say.

"So you waited until my sight was stolen to strike," said Spar. "Is that it?"

"More or less, although it won't be *I* who strikes you down," Gunmar answered. "I've reserved that pleasure for my heir."

Gunmar grunted, and a new Gumm-Gumm

strode into the chamber from the underground tunnel, dragging a barbaric broadsword behind him. He bore a striking resemblance to his much larger father, even if Spar could not see it. The Trollhunter's eyes did not move in their sockets as he felt a stabbing pain through his chest. The rest of Spar the Spiteful's body turned to solid stone and shattered into thousands of pieces.

"Well done, Bular," said Gunmar to his son.

"I know of no greater honor than to slay in your name, father," answered Bular.

Gunmar circled around his fallen nemesis, gloating, until a blue glow shone between the cracks of Spar's remains. The Amulet then burst out of the pile of rubble, flew past both Gumm-Gumms' clutching claws, and out of the cavern. Bular howled in outrage. He raked his claws along the carved walls, defiling them.

"No matter," said Gunmar. "Merlin's Amulet may have escaped us, but I now possess a far greater treasure! *The Book of—*"

Gunmar stopped short and snarled as he realized the Amulet wasn't the *only* thing to leave the ziggurat. His two burning eyes scoured the entire cavern and found no trace of *The Book of Ga-Huel* nor its bespectacled author.

"Bodus!" shouted Gunmar. "Come back here, you coward! You already know too much of my designs! Show me my future or forfeit your own!"

Across Sumer, Bodus shuddered at the echo of Gunmar's roars. The Troll adjusted his crystal specs and looked down at *The Book of Ga-Huel*. Its latest page showed Spar the Spiteful clutching at his eyes, two Gumm-Gumms lurking behind him. Tucking the book under his traveling cloak, Bodus fled into the night—into history—just as Merlin's Amulet soared the night sky in search of its next champion. . . .

CHAPTER 1
GUAC 'N' TROLL

Roughly 5,200 years later, Jim Lake Jr. held Merlin's Amulet in his young hands. He felt the device's inner workings tick and whir in his palm, sensing the full weight of his destiny. Clearing his mind and his heart, Jim read the mystical incantation inscribed upon the Amulet's back, and said, "For the glory of Merlin—LET'S GET THIS PARTY STARTED!"

Music thumped through the speakers. Carnival lights lit up Jim's backyard. A WELCOME HOME, JIMBO! banner unfurled. And Jim's best friends—Toby, Claire, Blinky, and AAARRRGGHH!!!—group-hugged their returned Trollhunter. Well, except for NotEnrique. The little Changeling wasn't too big on public displays of affection.

"Master Jim!" exclaimed Blinky, wiping the tears

from his six Troll eyes. "I can still scarcely believe that you managed to return from the Darklands—and alive, no less!"

"Glad to have you back," AAARRRGGHH!!! grumbled, tousling Jim's hair.

"You too, big guy," said Jim.

He hugged the giant Troll, happy to hear a heartbeat under all that muscle and fur. Jim reminded himself that it wasn't long ago that a poisoned blade had solidified AAARRRGGHH!!! into a lifeless statue, only for the spirits of past Trollhunters to revive him.

"We would've had this shindig a little earlier, if it wasn't for this week's Goblin trouble," Toby said, flashing a braces-filled grin.

"And under normal circumstances, we'd host this celebration at Trollmarket," added Blinky. "But I fear Queen Usurna wouldn't look kindly upon honoring the Trollhunter who defied her! Not to mention we don't have much in the way of human party snacks there. . . ."

"Eh, human food's overrated," said NotEnrique, scarfing down an old gym sock.

"Speaking of snacks, it's time to unlock the guac!" Claire announced.

She held out a bowl of her famous guacamole for the group. Jim dipped in a tortilla chip, took a bite, and closed his eyes. He chewed in silence, and Claire tried to read his reaction.

"Is it too bland?" she asked. "I can throw a ghost pepper in there for more heat! Or—"

"Claire," said Jim, opening his eyes and smiling. "It's perfect."

He hugged her, and his smile spread to the others. Jim looked around at his friends gathered in the backyard and added, "The guac, the decorations, the weather, the company—it's all *perfect*."

In truth, everything did seem perfect to Jim—especially when compared to what he endured in the Darklands. For two weeks Jim fought for his life in the dismal dimension. The only foods he had eaten there were raw Nyarlagroth eggs. The only banners he had seen were the war flags carried by two clashing armies. The only weather he had experienced was the mercilessly cold wind whipping against his Eclipse Armor. And the only company he had kept was the chalk drawing Jim made of his friends—that, and a talking fireball who betrayed Jim shortly before trying to kill him. Overall, it had been a pretty weird time for the Trollhunter.

The sounds of his teammates' laughter roused Jim back to the present. Blinky hoisted a glass of glug into the air and said, "And now, in the immortal words of the Venerable Bedehilde: Yo, DJ! Pump up the jamz!"

NotEnrique popped a vinyl record onto the turntable and cranked up the volume. A blistering Papa Skull track flooded the yard, and Team Trollhunters started dancing. Claire giggled at Jim's patented "thumbs-up groove." Blinky popped and locked with all four of his arms. And Toby cheered on AAARRRGGHH!!!, who had picked up a lot of moves from their *Go-Go Dance Uprising* video game.

"Go Wingman! Go Wingman! It's your birthday!" said Toby.

"What is the meaning of this?!" yelled someone from across the yard.

The record needle scratched, and everybody stopped dancing. At first Jim thought they must've been found out by a neighbor with a noise complaint. How was Jim going to explain to his mom that he was throwing a house party while she worked a night shift at the hospital? Or that he was secretly living a double life as an armored, magically powered champion? Or that Jim had already erased the truth about his Trollhunting from her memory once before? But before Jim could come up with a lame excuse, the party crasher stepped closer. The twinkling carnival lights revealed a blue, broad, and spiked Troll.

"Draal!" Jim hollered.

"How can you possibly have a party . . . without *these*?" said Draal, pulling his mechanical arm from behind his back to reveal three plump watermelons.

"Oh, it's on," Jim said. "For the glory of Merlin, Daylight is mine to command!"

The Amulet floated before Jim and released swarming orbs of pale blue energy. Interlocking metal plates manifested out of the thin air and contracted around Jim's body, sheathing him in radiant armor. The Trollhunter gestured, and the Sword of Daylight appeared in his awaiting hand.

Draal hurled all three of the melons. In one fluid stroke, Jim slashed through each of them, splattering the rest of Team Trollhunters with melon chunks. They looked at one another in startled silence—then burst into applause.

"Now *that's* how you party," said Draal.

"Hey, Draal, any more where those came from?" asked Toby, pulling a small hammer from his back pocket.

The spiked Troll winked before rolling over to the garden bed, where Jim grew organic fruits, vegetables, and herbs to be used in his cooking. Draal peered between shrubs of thyme and rosemary, finding a fourth, much larger watermelon. He cocked a metal thumbs up to the group, and Toby extended his Warhammer to its full, formidable size. Knowing what was coming next, Jim, Claire, Blinky, and AAARRRGGHH!!! hid behind one of the boulders in the backyard and giggled.

"Batter up!" yelled Toby.

As Draal launched the melon like a cannonball, Toby swung his Warhammer with everything he had, the weapon's crystal head trailing amber fire in the night air. The watermelon exploded in a thunderclap of fruit and flame, and the shockwaves sent Toby flying rear-first into Jim's trash cans. With melon juice raining down, NotEnrique cueing a new song, and everyone else hoisting the woozy Toby on their shoulders, Jim felt like he wanted this moment to last forever. The Trollhunter pumped his fists into the air and shouted, "This is the greatest night of my life!"

Much later that night—after his guests had picked the last melon seeds from their hair and fur, and left—Jim went to sleep with a smile still on his face. But when he heard a strange sound and opened his eyes, Jim discovered he wasn't in his bedroom anymore.

He was back in the Darklands. In place of pajamas, Jim now wore the black-and-red Eclipse Armor. Frigid gales whipped his exposed hair, and a photonegative sun shone sickly green light upon the jagged terrain.

"Oh no," moaned Jim. "I can't be back here! I—I don't ever want to be back here!"

Overcome with dread, Jim took a step backward, only for the ground to crumble beneath his feet. Jim cried out as he plunged through darkness. He thought he might die this way, falling forever, until the Trollhunter's open hand caught something.

It was a chain. The abrupt stop made Jim's shoulder pop out of its socket, but he still managed to hold on to the rusted metal links. Mustering all his strength, Jim pulled himself up the chain. Even the slightest movement sent an agonizing throb running down his arm, but he refused to let go. Blinking away tears, Jim's eyes refocused and saw that he was now clinging on to a bassinet.

"The Changeling nursery!" he gasped.

Jim then heard a baby start to cry. The wail came from everywhere and nowhere at once. His armored hand reached into the bassinet, peeling back the blankets. But the more Jim pulled on the fabric, the more folds it seemed to reveal. The bleating cries grew louder, drowning out the sound of the Jim's pounding heartbeat. He finally tore off the last blanket. And the very sight of the horror he unveiled made the Trollhunter scream.

Jim's eyes snapped open. He was back in his room, drenched in sweat, jaws clenched. His arm had gone numb, not from a dislocated shoulder, but from sleeping awkwardly on it.

"Whew," sighed Jim, feeling the nightmare fading already. "What was in that guac?"

The alarm clock read 2:00 a.m. There were

still four more hours before he had to wake up for school. Relieved, Jim went back to sleep—only to sit upright in bed all of a sudden and yell, "Holy sheesh-kabobs! I forgot my homework!"

CHAPTER 2

ACCIDENTS HAPPEN

A black hole opened in front of the lockers at Arcadia Oaks High School. Claire stepped out, yawning, and said, "You guys coming?"

Toby practically sleepwalked out of the vortex. Jim followed his best friend out, saying, "Sorry, guys. I shouldn't have bothered you with this."

"Hey, after two weeks of no Jim, we'll take all the time we can get with you," said Claire.

"Even if it's at school," Toby added drowsily. "And way before first period."

Jim dialed the combination to his locker and said, "If it's any consolation, I should have just enough time to finish my Algebra homework and turn it—"

The sound of raised voices made Jim stop talking. He, Claire, and Toby all turned their heads and looked down the empty hall. Two people spoke again from inside one of the classrooms. Jim strained to make out the words, but they were muffled and indistinct.

"What language is that?" Toby asked.

"I don't know," Claire admitted. "But whatever it is, it sure sounds heated."

They crept down the hallway and stopped just outside of Señor Uhl's Spanish class. They could see his silhouette pacing in front of the door's frosted glass and hear his German accent.

". . . completely unacceptable!" growled Señor Uhl. "They must step up the timetable!"

Jim, Toby, and Claire stared at one another and mouthed the same word: "Timetable?"

"The return will happen as planned," argued another person with a different accent.

Curious to get a look at the second person in Uhl's class, Toby stood on his tiptoes and peered into the window. But his sneakers were still wet with melon juice, making the rubber soles squeak loudly against the linoleum floor. Uhl's outline went ramrod straight.

"What is it? Why have you stopped talking?" asked the foreign voice.

"Shh," said Uhl. "There may be a spy in our midst. . . ."

The trio of eavesdroppers scrambled away as Uhl opened the door and poked his flat-topped head into the hall. Around the corner, Claire, Toby, and Jim flattened against the wall and held their breaths. Seeing nothing but vacant hallway, Uhl returned to his class and shut the door.

"Did you see who Señor Uhl was arguing with?" whispered Jim.

"No, the only body I saw in there was his musclebound one," Toby whispered back.

But before any of them could say another word, an unexpected glow caught their attention. They looked across the hall, where eerie lights danced behind another door.

"That . . . that's Strickler's old office," stammered Claire.

"I thought you sent him packing on a one-way ride to Nowheresville," Toby said.

"I did," answered Jim, his face flushing with anger.

He marched over to Strickler's erstwhile office and flung open the door, causing even more mysterious light to flood into the hallway. The

Trollhunter and his friends shielded their eyes.

"All right, *Walter*, what're you doing back in Arcadia?" Jim shouted into the glare. "Just because you gave me Gunmar's Eye doesn't mean you get a second chance with my mom or—"

And just like that, the light vanished. The teens lowered their arms. Other than the three of them, Walter Strickler's office remained completely empty. Toby said, "Maybe he installed some of those ultra-bright LED bulbs before skipping town?"

"That light didn't come from any bulb, Tobes," said Jim. "It came from over there."

Jim pointed to Strickler's desk and the old, leather-bound tome left open on its surface.

"It's *The Book of Ga-Huel*," remembered Claire. "Tobes, we must've forgotten to put it away the last time we were here."

"In our defense, Angor Rot *was* trying to murder us and all," argued Toby.

Jim ran his fingers against the book's open pages and said, "For an ancient book of Gumm-Gumm history, the ink still feels pretty fresh."

"I could've sworn those pages were blank last time," Claire said.

"Ah, the AC probably kicked on and blew it open to a different page," Toby reasoned, hearing a faint hiss in the ceiling air-conditioner vent.

"Maybe," Jim said. "But that still doesn't explain why a book that's thousands of years old is suddenly glowing in a deserted school office. Right?"

Claire said, "That sounds like a Blinky question. We should get this to him right away."

Toby was about to chime in with his agreement when the hissing grew louder. He spotted something moving behind the vent's metal grill and swallowed hard. Jim and Claire followed Toby's blanched gaze, seeing a column of deep, purple smoke bloom out of the duct.

"Antramonstrum!" Jim yelled to his friends. "Don't let it touch you!"

Jim had seen up close the kind of damage wreaked by these sentient death clouds during his tour of duty in the Darklands. He had watched in horror as an Antramonstrum passed over a platoon of Gumm-Gumm soldiers, leaving only their fossilized husks in its wake.

The sounds of Toby and Claire extending their Warhammer and Shadow Staff pulled Jim back into the present. The Antramonstrum surged over to the book shelf in Strickler's office and swirled around a pink crystal. Claire said, "It . . . it looks like it's trying to get inside that crystal."

"Only Mr. Toxic-Gas-Giant doesn't seem to be having much luck," quipped Toby.

The Antramonstrum prodded the crystal repeatedly, but only succeeded in knocking it to the floor, where it shattered. Even though it had no lungs, the smoke creature still shrieked in anguish. The three friends covered their ears, until the Antramonstrum's screech abated.

Jim said, "That thing's louder than the school bell! We gotta shut it up before Uhl hears!"

Claire nodded and summoned a new black hole below the Antramonstrum. But its violet, vaporous body started to drift away from the portal.

"Tobes, use your Warhammer to weigh it down!" said Jim.

A knowing, metal-mouthed grin spread across Toby's face. He jammed the hammerhead into the Antramonstrum's billowing form and concentrated. The Warhammer's energies seeped into the writhing smoke, condensing the cloud, increasing its gravity.

The Antramonstrum sank lower and lower—and closer and closer to Claire's portal. Toby and Claire poured everything they had into their weapons until the Antramonstrum dropped like a stone into the black hole.

"Whoa. Heavy," said Toby as Claire closed the portal.

Jim tucked *The Book of Ga-Huel* next to the Amulet in his backpack just as the first bell rang. Claire cracked open the office door, revealing droves of students now flowing through the halls. Sighing, Jim said, "So much for getting my homework done. Ms. Janeth's gonna kill me."

"Want me to pretend to be you again, like when you were in the Darklands?" asked Toby, pulling an odd, Tiki-like mask out of his own backpack. "I've still got the Glamour Mask!"

"No thanks, Tobes," said Jim. "My grades are *still* on life support from last time."

Toby shrugged and said, "Too bad they don't give out *A*s for impersonation. This mask made me look and sound so much like you, not even your mom could tell the difference!"

"Let's go. Uhl's giving detentions to anyone he catches in off-limits areas," Claire said.

They exited Strickler's office and merged with the flow of hallway traffic—only for Jim to immediately collide with someone carrying a teetering stack of textbooks.

"I'm so sorry!" Jim said as he helped collect the books. "I wasn't watching where I . . ."

Jim trailed off. A redheaded woman in her twenties stood across from him, holding out her arms to accept the books. She smiled dazzlingly and said, "No biggie. Accidents happen!"

Toby stood riveted next to Jim. They both stared at her with matching dopey grins, absentmindedly holding her books. The redhead still held out her arms, but the guys just kept staring. Claire cleared her throat, reviving Jim, who hastily returned the textbooks.

"Are you new here?" Toby asked the woman, his eyes still glazed. "You look new. I haven't seen you before. I'd remember that. You must be new. Are you new here?"

"Yes, siree, I am!" she said with a snorting laugh. "Sorry, I snort when I'm nervous."

"Nervous?" said Jim. "Why in the world would you be nervous? About anything? Ever?"

Claire shot Jim a dirty look as the woman said, "Oh, it's my first day on the job. I'm your new school librarian, Eloise Stemhower."

"Eloise," Toby repeated in a singsong way.

"Well, Ellie for short," said Ellie. "I mean, 'Eloise' sounds so old-fashioned. I don't know *what* my mom was thinking when she named me. Other than 'What kind of name will guarantee my daughter grows up to become a school librarian?'"

Jim and Toby both laughed extremely loudly at the joke. Ellie joined in with more of her snorting, until the second bell rang.

"Uh-oh. I think that means I'm late!" Ellie yelped. "See ya in the stacks!"

Jim and Toby kept smiling even after Ellie passed through the library door. Claire shook her head and muttered, "Ugh. I think I'd rather be with that mindless Antramonstrum than you two *boys*. . . ."

CHAPTER 3
A REAL PAGE-TURNER

Seven grueling periods of high school later, Jim and Toby found themselves *still* apologizing to Claire as she shadow-jumped them into Blinky's Troll library.

"—we were just welcoming Ellie, Claire!" Jim said. "Like . . . like school ambassadors!"

Their sudden appearance made Blinky—who'd been standing on AAARRRGGHH!!!'s head to reach some scrolls on the tallest shelf—lose his balance and come crashing down with a loud "Yaaaaah!"

"Ambassadors who can't stop drooling, you mean," said Claire. "Sorry, Blinky. My bad."

"My drooling has nothing to do with how Ellie's freckles seem to twinkle like a constellation of heavenly stars whenever she smiles," Toby protested. "For all you know, it's related to an ongoing orthodontic condition!"

"Orka-donka?" AAARRRGGHH!!! mispronounced as he helped Blinky out of the unspooled scrolls.

"*Orthodontic*," Blinky clarified. "A specialized field of dentistry designed to straighten humans' teeth for some inane reason."

"It won't seem so inane when I get my braces off in another decade or so," said Toby.

"Which is about as long as it'll take to clean this mess," Blinky muttered, gesturing to the scrolls.

"Don't worry, Blink. We'll help. And maybe *this* will make it up to you," said Jim as he unzipped his backpack and pulled out . . .

"*The Book of Ga-Huel*!" exclaimed Blinky.

He raced over to Jim and gingerly took the tome from his hands. The leather binding creaked as Blinky opened the book and ran his sixteen fingers along the arcane script and sketches contained within.

"Sorta like *A Brief Recapitulation of Gumm-Gumm Lore*, huh?" joked Jim.

"Just so, Master Jim," Blinky confirmed. "The Gumm-Gumm's former king, Orlagk the Oppressor, commissioned it after learning of the Venerable Bedehilde's forty-seven volume magnum opus."

"Sounds like a real page-turner," Toby said sarcastically.

"That it is, Tobias," concurred Blinky. "For legend holds that this book does not just chronicle the history of the Gumm-Gumm empire—but also its *future*."

Jim, Claire, Toby, and AAARRRGGHH!!! all raised their eyebrows, impressed.

"The story goes that Orlagk learned of a traitor in his ranks, a soldier who dared to overthrow him and take control of the Gumm-Gumm army," Blinky went on.

"Gunmar," said Jim, based on the firsthand account he'd heard in the Darklands.

"Correct, Master Jim!" answered Blinky. "Though Gunmar was careful to keep his mutinous plans secret at the time. Growing desperate, Orlagk turned to forbidden, dark magic to help him root out the true identity of his eventual betrayer. Thus was born *The Book of Ga-Huel*."

"But if Orlagk ordered the book's creation, why didn't he use it to expose Gunmar and save his own life?" asked Claire.

"Unfortunately, the answer to that mystery

has been lost to time, fair Claire," said Blinky. "Throughout the ages, many Trollhunters have endeavored to track down the book and use its valuable knowledge for good, rather than evil. But *The Book of Ga-Huel* has always managed to slip out of their grasp time and time again."

"Until *now*," added AAARRRGGHH!!!

"You mean, we could use this book to get a sneak peek at where our enemies are gonna attack before it even happens?" said Claire, her voice rising in excitement.

"Or the answers to next week's chemistry quiz?" asked Toby.

"Why, yes, Claire," realized Blinky. "And forget about it, Domzalski."

AAARRRGGHH!!! looked over to Jim, who stayed unusually quiet. He seemed lost in thought, as if some little detail was nagging at the edge of his memory.

"Jim okay?" asked the gentle giant.

"Yeah, I'm fine," Jim said unconvincingly. "It's just . . . there's something else the book might be able to tell us."

Jim felt all his friends' eyes turn toward him.

He tried to organize his scattered thoughts as best he could and said, "That Antramonstrum. Back at Strickler's. It looked like it was trying to get back into that crystal, didn't it?"

Blinky and AAARRRGGHH!!! watched Toby and Claire nod in unison.

"And Tobes, you told me that the Antramonstrum that attacked you, Blink, and AAARRRGGHH!!! months ago came out of a crystal in Strickler's office," Jim went on.

"Yeah, it did," said Toby. "Before we sucked it into the Darklands through that Fetch."

"Exactly!" Jim said, snapping his fingers. "So what I'm wondering is: What if that was the *same* Antramonstrum we fought today? What if it followed me back to Arcadia and tried to return to its crystal home? And what if it wasn't alone when it escaped the Darklands?"

The members of Team Trollhunters stared at one another in mounting dread. Jim's voice tightened with nerves as he added, "What if Gunmar got out, too? Could *The Book of Ga-Huel* show us where to find him?"

"You raise a most troubling series of questions

indeed, Master Jim," said Blinky, who began fanning through the blank pages at the back. "Though the answers should be easy enough to obtain. All we need do is turn to the very last chapters of *The Book of Ga-Huel* and—"

"No!" cried Jim, Toby, and Claire.

They knocked the book out of Blinky's hand a split second before one of the blank pages unleashed an intensely bright beam. Claire used her Shadow Staff to generate a protective shade around her light-sensitive Troll friends. Holding his hand in front of his eyes, Jim peeked between his fingers and saw new words and pictures start to fill the illuminated page. A moment later, the blinding glow stopped as suddenly as it had started.

"By Gorgus!" marveled Blinky.

He tapped the corner of the book with his foot. No more light flashed, so Blinky figured it was safe to handle. He picked up the tome, looked at the now-filled page, and cried, "Great Gronka Morka!"

Shaken, Blinky threw the book back onto the floor. Jim and the others rushed to him, inspecting his many limbs for any sign of injury.

"Blink, what is it?" asked Jim. "Are you hurt?"

"No," Blinky said in a dry rasp. "Although it appears that's about to change. Look!"

All four of his hands pointed to the Troll library floor, where the book had landed open once again. Everyone else's eyes all went as wide as Blinky's. For *The Book of Ga-Huel*'s newest page now featured an ink drawing of Jim, Claire, Toby, AAARRRGGHH!!!, and Draal all standing in mourning around the broken, stony remains of Blinky's dead body.

CHAPTER 4

BA-BRU-AH'S BODYGUARD

Doctor Barbara Lake wanted to scream.

After thirty-six hours of back-to-back shifts at Arcadia Oaks Hospital—and an extra forty-five minutes of traffic on the ride home—Jim's mom had reached the end of her patience. She slid her key into the front door, entered her house, and kicked off her clogs. Barbara saw the framed wall photo of Jim as a toddler and immediately started feeling better.

"Jim, I'm home," she called from the foyer. "How was school today?"

In the basement directly beneath Barbara, Draal stopped sharpening his ax. He had been scraping a whetstone against his prized weapon, honing its blade to razor-sharpness. But now the spiked Troll remained quiet as Barbara's footsteps crossed over his head. Draal listened to her walk through the dining room and into the kitchen.

"Jim? Honey? Are you upstairs?" Draal heard Barbara say through the floorboards. "If you're doing your homework, I can help! For the first time since fourth grade . . ."

Barbara muttered that last part under her breath. But Draal had cupped his hand around his ear, and his heightened Troll hearing picked up every last syllable. By now, he knew what would come next. Barbara would realize that Jim was out of the house, that she missed him yet again. Then she would bury her face in her hands and curse herself for not being there enough for her son—for not being present during these important teenage years. But Barbara would then take a deep breath, promise herself she'd do better next time, and try to cook dinner on her own before ultimately burning the food.

Draal rested his ax on the cold basement floor and listened to Barbara go through her entire guilty cycle: cursing, breathing, promising, and cooking. A minute later Draal heard the kitchen smoke alarm go off, right on schedule. The Troll lumbered over to the window set high in the basement wall, which looked onto the backyard. Through the narrow glass pane, Draal saw Barbara's bare feet dash into the twilit lawn. She ran over to the trash can—which now sported a rump-shaped dent in its side, courtesy of Toby—and scraped the charred, smoking "dinner" out of her frying pan.

"Better luck next time, Ba-Bru-Ah," Draal said quietly.

Despite himself, Draal could not help but feel sorry for Jim's mother. He had sworn to protect Barbara to his dying day, much as he swore devout allegiance to the Trollhunter for sparing Draal's life. The spiked Troll treated this bodyguard duty as the most important job of his very long existence, and intended to keep it just that—a job. But after months of secretly living in their basement, Draal had overheard how much Jim and Barbara truly loved each other. Their special bond often made Draal think about his own mother, Ballustra, and how much he missed her.

He sniffled and wiped his nose. Draal then considered the replacement hand he just used and the larger prosthetic connected to it. Curling the metal fingers into a fist, he remembered how he'd literally given his right arm months ago to free Merlin's Amulet from the reassembled Killahead Bridge. At the time, Draal hadn't paid much thought to the consequences before leaping into action, just as he hadn't missed his pulverized appendage ever since. Losing an arm to abort Gunmar's return to the surface world seemed a reasonable sacrifice to Draal. And even though he occasionally felt phantom pains of the Amulet searing into his former palm, Draal would gladly offer his left arm and both legs, too, if it meant protecting the Trollhunter and his family.

Barbara's sudden shriek made Draal look up again. His eyes scoped the backyard for danger, then rested on Barbara's bare feet again. She lifted one of them, revealing squishy bits of melon between her toes. Draal's posture relaxed. They must've missed a spot during their cleanup.

"Gross," Barbara grumbled. "What in the *world* was Jim up to out here?"

Draal's smirk faded when he saw something out of the corner of his eye. A pair of unmistakably yellow eyes watched Barbara from the shadows at the far end of the yard. Alarmed, Draal pressed his face against the window. But the glass had been spotted with water stains from the lawn sprinklers, making it impossible to get a better look.

Barbara hosed off her feet, oblivious to the stranger skulking in the periphery. Those eyes seemed to get bigger as their owner took a step toward Jim's mom. Draal grabbed his ax and ran for the stairs before skidding to a halt. If he were to run into the yard now, he'd reveal his existence to Barbara. But if he did nothing, then the life of the Trollhunter's mother would be in jeopardy. Draal's mind raced as he debated what to do.

Outside, Barbara shut off the hose, still unaware of the presence behind her. Draal finally tucked his body into a spiked blue ball and rolled up the basement steps as Barbara opened the back door. Timing it just right, Draal wheeled onto the staircase to the second floor, while Barbara entered her kitchen. Draal continued into Jim's bedroom before launching his rounded form out of the open window.

Now in the living room, Barbara could no longer

see her backyard—or the brawny, ax-wielding Troll that just landed in it. Draal slashed blindly at the shadows, but his blade passed only through bushes and branches. He stopped and studied the entire perimeter of the yard. It was empty, save for Draal—and a very startled raccoon in the oak tree.

CHAPTER 5
FIGHT THE FUTURE

"So I says: *'Kelpestrum?!* It darn near *killed* 'em!'" joked NotEnrique.

Gnome Chompsky squeaked with laughter as he and the little Changeling barged into the Troll library. But the miniature pair fell silent when they saw Blinky huddled in the corner, shaking his head and moaning "Great Gronka Morka" over and over again.

"Neep, neep, neep?" asked Chompsky.

"Yeah, what's with him?" NotEnrique repeated, jerking his tiny green thumb at Blinky.

Jim, Toby, and Claire looked up from *The Book of Ga-Huel* at the new arrivals. As AAARRRGGHH!!! tenderly draped a blanket over Blinky's shoulders, the Trollhunter said, "Let's just say that *The Book of Ga-Huel* isn't the feel-good read of the year. Or millennium."

Gnome Chompsky removed his hat, revealing his broken horn, and chittered in agitation.

"You said it," NotEnrique agreed. "There's some bad juju in them pages."

"Yes, terrible juju! The very worst juju!" said Blinky, getting to his feet. "Forgive me, my friends. But when confronted with the bleak portent of my own demise, I'm afraid I—"

"Freaked out?" offered Toby.

"Went crazy-town banana-pants?" offered Claire.

"With extra side of nuts?" offered AAARRRGGHH!!!

"All the above, I suppose," said Blinky, returning the blanket to AAARRRGGHH!!! "It's just that, in spite of recent adversities, these past few months have been among the finest of my long life. Masters Jim, Tobias, and Claire—you have blessed me with your trust and friendship. And AAARRRGGHH!!!, to have you among the living once again . . ."

His voice grew thick with emotion, and his six eyes welled with tears. Chompsky locked the library doors, figuring the last thing they all needed now was any more unannounced visitors.

"Believe me, I know *just* how you feel, Blink," Jim reassured. "But don't worry. Team Trollhunters is finally back together, and we won't let anything break us apart again."

"It sounded like you knew about this book," Claire said to NotEnrique. "Anything important you can share with the rest of us?"

"Only what I overheard the Janus Order reporting through the Fetch portals while I was livin' in the Darklands," he answered.

"The Janus Order! Of course that network of Changeling spies would be involved in this," hissed Blinky. "Those two-faced shape-shifters bring nothing but misery and death—er, present company excluded, NotEnrique."

The reformed Changeling shrugged and said, "None taken! Those snobby twits refused my application when I tried to join 'em! And it's not like it matters anyway. The Order's kept that book under lock and key since 1937, but hardly any of the agents had enough gronk-nuks to actually go near the bloody thing. Strickler was the only one who could ever read it and not turn as white as a Blood Goblin's bottom. So when he decided to move it to his office at yer school, nobody put up a fight."

"But just because something shows up in *The Book of Ga-Huel* doesn't necessarily mean it's gonna happen . . . right?" asked Toby.

With a sullen expression, Blinky took the book from Claire and opened it. Jim shouted, "Blinky, no! That light blast will turn you into—"

"I am heartened by your concern, Master Jim," said Blinky. "But I believe that light only emanates once blank pages are filled with new writings. Otherwise, I would've been turned to stone when I first encountered these accursed annals in Strickler's office, lo those many months ago. Besides, if we treat the book's contents as fact—and I believe we must—then no harm will befall me in my library. That page I saw of . . . of my own *death* . . . took place in an entirely different setting. Also, Draal appears in that dreadful drawing, yet he is not present here."

Blinky licked his finger and pored through the book's earliest chapters. His many eyes took in the strange symbols and savage imagery. Turning from page to page, Blinky winced anew at each entry in this history of horrors. He saw the page illustrating Spar the Spiteful's final moments with Gunmar and Bular. Another page documented how Gunmar betrayed Orlagk the Oppressor, losing an eye in the process. And yet another recounted AAARRRGGHH!!!'s change of heart at the Battle of Killahead Bridge, followed by Gunmar's exile to the Darklands. With a weary breath, Blinky shut *The Book of Ga-Huel* and felt a desperate need to wash his four hands.

"As you can see, Tobias, every event depicted within its chapters has, in fact, come to pass," Blink continued with some difficulty. "For whatever purpose, we have been given a glimpse of the future. And its course appears rather fixed."

"We can't think like that, Blink," said Jim, even as he felt the Amulet tick in his pocket like a doomsday clock. "We've faced so many other insane challenges and won each time. If we have to fight the future, then so be it."

"And since all we have right now are questions, we should start by answering them," suggested Claire. "Like, *how* can a book predict the future in the first place?"

"And *who* is the ghost writer still adding pages across time and space?" Toby added.

"I . . . I don't know," Jim confessed. "But I think I know who might—"

Three loud bangs at the library doors made everyone freeze in place. They all watched the deadbolt rattle as three more knocks thundered from the other side.

"Blinkous Galadrigal and Aarghaumont of the Krubera!" said Queen Usurna. "By the order of the Troll Tribunal, I demand you open these doors and surrender your human Trollhunter for further questioning."

"Man, you really are Panama-nun-grotto around here," Toby whispered to Jim.

"*Persona non grata,*" Blinky corrected. "It means an unwelcome person who—"

"I hear voices in there!" boomed Queen Usurna. "Enough delaying. You Kruberas break down these doors at once. So commands your queen!"

Heavy Troll fists and shoulders banged against the library doors harder than before. Claire focused her attention on the Shadow Staff and opened another black vortex. Jim, Toby, Blinky, and AAARRRGGHH!!! each ran through it, while NotEnrique and Chompsky lagged behind. Claire beckoned them forward as the deadbolt started to crack. But NotEnrique shooed her away with a wave and whispered, "We got this, sis."

Claire nodded at the little green imp and disappeared into her portal just as the doors crashed down. A battalion of Krubera Trolls flooded into the library, followed by Queen Usurna, her regal head upturned in disdain. NotEnrique stood before her, talking into a scroll like it was a microphone, while Chompsky rolled on the floor in laughter.

"Ah, I see we got some guests from outta town!" NotEnrique said to the Kruberas. "Speakin' of outta town, anyone here ever been to Gatto's Keep? It's more like Gatto's *Seep*, amiright?! I mean, what's the deal with that Mountain Troll's digestive system? Pee-yew!"

Chompsky doubled over in hysterics, but Usurna seemed less than entertained. She turned on her heels and strode out of the library, followed by her confused Krubera soldiers.

"Hey, you guys've been a fun crowd!" NotEnrique called after them as they left the library in a huff. "Drive safely and don't forget to tip yer Gnomes on the way out!"

CHAPTER 6
SEEKING COUNCIL

Jim could've sworn he heard the distant hiss of Strickler's Antramonstrum as he and his friends crossed through the Shadow Realm. The Trollhunter wondered whether the smoke creature preferred being exiled here or in the Darklands. In the end, though, Jim decided both places were pretty terrible. He shuddered and watched Claire conjure another portal, depositing them into Trollmarket's training pit—the Hero's Forge.

"We better move quickly," said Claire. "Who knows how long NotEnrique's diversion will keep Queen Usurna occupied."

AAARRRGGHH!!! pulled a lever in one of the arena's recesses. Enormous gears cranked behind the sheer rock walls, and the foreboding relic known as the Soothscryer emerged.

"You sure you wanna put your arm in there, Jimbo?" asked Toby. "The last things I saw go into the Soothscryer were those PyroBligst gorbs. And they never came out again!"

"I have to, Tobes," said Jim. "It's the only way I can reach the Void."

"And the Council of Trollhunters," concluded Blinky.

"It's like you mentioned earlier, Blink," Jim said. "Trollhunters throughout time have tried to locate and understand *The Book of Ga-Huel*, only to turn up empty-handed."

"But together, their spirits may have enough collective information to piece together a bigger picture—a greater understanding of how its fortune-telling powers work!" said Blinky, catching on. "One which might . . . might . . ."

"Save Blinky," AAARRRGGHH!!! finished.

Jim raised his Amulet and said, "For the glory of Merlin, Daylight is mine to command!"

The incantation triggered the Daylight Armor to materialize around Jim. He gave Blinky an encouraging thumbs-up with one armored hand while thrusting the other into the Soothscryer's open jaws. Jim shut his eyes and felt a powerfully old magic overtake his body, pulling him forward. When he reopened them, Jim found himself in an entirely different—but no less disorienting—landscape than the Shadow Realm.

"The Void," Jim said, his voice echoing along the afterlife's misty expanse.

He had not spent much time here before, but being back in the Void made Jim's pulse race with a blend of nerves and excitement. It reminded him of the feeling he got before taking a big test at school—a feeling of being watched and judged all at the same time.

Numerous spheres of energy flew out of the Void's haze and approached Jim. One by one, the incandescent balls expanded and took shape. Jim looked on in awe, soon finding himself surrounded by the Council of Trollhunters. Each of these spirits had served in turn as Merlin's champions. And once their bodies had fallen (almost always in battle), their souls had then ascended to this rarified plane.

"Um, hey," said Jim lamely to the impassive Trollhunters.

Some of the transparent figures shifted aside, making way for two of the finest warriors to ever wield Daylight—Kanjigar the Courageous and Deya the Deliverer.

"Well met, Trollhunter," greeted Kanjigar. "Do not mistake our silence for displeasure. And yet we know your appearance here is of grave import."

Deya stared disarmingly into Jim's eyes and said, "Forsooth, we have witnessed your recent woes from the Void. We already understand what—and who—lies in the balance."

"Then you can help me save Blinky!" Jim said hopefully.

"That remains to be *seen*, human," said the spirit of Spar the Spiteful.

Jim could tell from the faraway gaze in Spar's eyes that he was still blinded in the afterlife. Another Trollhunter, a Krubera like AAARRRGGHH!!!, took a step forward and gave Jim a hearty slap on the back. Caught off guard, Jim stumbled forward and wondered how he could've felt that in a place populated entirely by ghosts.

"Greetings, flesh child!" said the Krubera Trollhunter with a bemused laugh. "I am Boraz the Bold! Surely you recognize me from the many statues, songs, and sagas made in my honor?"

"Um . . . sure?" lied Jim.

"Naturally!" Boraz the Bold said without actually stopping to listen. "Then you are no doubt aware of how I inherited the Amulet from Spar after he was felled by that Gumm-Gumm scum. But did you know that I, Boraz the Bold, *also* encountered *The Book of Ga-Huel* during one of my many memorable conquests?"

Before Jim could answer, Boraz laughed another haughty laugh and said, "It's a trick question. Of course you knew. Who *doesn't* know about Boraz the Bold's every adventure?!"

Jim turned back toward Kanjigar and Deya for help, but they merely shrugged in a "What can you do?" fashion. Boraz wrapped one muscular arm around Jim's shoulders while gesturing grandly to the horizon with his free hand.

"Except it's one thing to hear about my greatness and another thing entirely to *see* it," Boraz continued. "So come with me—Boraz the Bold—and witness history in the making! Would that make my little fan happy?"

Before Jim could correct Boraz, he realized they were no longer standing in the Void—or the Hero's Forge for that matter. Instead, the pair of Trollhunters stood in an altogether different arena, yet one that seemed strangely familiar to Jim.

"Welcome to the famed Colosseum of Rome!" said Boraz the Bold.

Jim grimaced as the former Trollhunter let out another self-satisfied laugh. But Jim instantly knew Boraz was right. He recognized the iconic structure from the AP World History class Strickler used to teach. Only, this Colosseum looked brand-new and empty, like it hadn't yet been used. He ran his armored fingers over the smooth limestone pillars and could practically smell wet stucco on the walls.

"Unreal," said Jim.

He remembered how one page in their textbooks featured two side-by-side images: The first was a photograph of the Colosseum's weathered ruins as they appeared in Jim's era. The second was an artists' rendering of what the famous stadium would have looked like in its heyday. Standing there now, Jim could see that the artist was off on certain details about the height of the spectator stands and the orientation of the gladiator pens.

"I'd hazard we're here circa the year 70 CE on your funny human calendar," said Boraz. "Actually, I know for a fact it's 70 CE because that's when . . . well, you'll see!"

Moonlight shined down through the Colosseum's open-air arena. Jim noticed how it reflected off their armor and asked, "Boraz, are . . . are we actually here?"

"HA!" roared Boraz. "Only in spirit, small one. In these Void Visitations, we may observe what has transpired. But none may see, hear, or touch us. And it's 'the Bold.' Boraz the Bold. Say it with me. Boraz the Bold."

"Boraz the Bold," Jim said halfheartedly.

"There! You're getting the hang of it!" Boraz the Bold said cheerfully. "Look!"

Jim followed Boraz the Bold's pointing finger to one of the gladiator pens. Its gates burst open from the inside, and out strutted . . . another Boraz the Bold.

"That's . . . that's you!" said Jim to the ghost of Boraz the Bold beside him.

"Great Gorgus, I'd almost forgotten how good I

looked!" said Boraz's spirit. "Now watch this part. Watch what I do here!"

Jim watched as the living Boraz the Bold threw a potbellied, bespectacled Troll over his shoulder and leaped from the pens to the middle of the Colosseum.

"Watch it, Trollhunter!" cried Bodus, nearly dropping *The Book of Ga-Huel* onto the arena's sandy floor. "You're meant to save my life—not prematurely end it!"

Dozens of Gumm-Gumms chased after them. They hurled their Parlok Spears at the squealing Bodus, but Boraz the Bold dodged each volley with admirable skill. The spirit version of Boraz winked at Jim and said, "Bet you can't do that."

A Gumm-Gumm roared, "For once, we have no quarrel with you, Trollhunter! Hand over the Dishonorable Bodus so that our general, Gunmar the Black, might discuss his last rites!"

Both Boraz the Bolds threw back their heads and laughed at the same time. The living Boraz on the field started talking to the Gumm-Gumms. But Jim noticed how the ghostly Boraz beside him mouthed the exact same words, as if he had memorized them.

"—and that's why Boraz the Bold will never yield to you! Ever! No matter who gets caught in the crossfire!" said the living Boraz before jumping back into the Gumm-Gumm mob.

"What're you doing?!" shrieked Bodus. "Gunmar wants to kill me for every prophecy I've ever foretold—especially my latest one about the Triumbric Stones!"

If the Trollhunter of 70 CE understood what Bodus was saying, he never showed it. He simply roared with another vainglorious laugh and set about subduing the Gumm-Gumms. Boraz the Bold defeated one enemy soldier after another, all while Bodus kicked and screamed in protest. Jim noticed Boraz's spirit shadow-boxing beside him and, for a moment, it looked like the corporeal Boraz might actually win this gladiatorial Troll fight.

But then one of the battered Gumm-Gumms got to his feet again and hurled his Parlok Spear, stabbing the Dishonorable Bodus in the back. Within seconds, the author's body slipped off the Trollhunter's and shattered into thousands of pieces on the Colosseum floor. Boraz the Bold—both versions of him—could only watch as the

Gumm-Gumms retrieved *The Book of Ga-Huel* from the pile of rubble and escaped into the arena's warren of underground tunnels.

"Well, I think my work here is done," said Boraz's spirit as his younger self began digging a grave.

"Your work?!" Jim exclaimed in disbelief. "Boraz, you let Bodus get killed and *The Book of Ga-Huel* fall into Gunmar's hands! You didn't *do* anything!"

"First of all, it's Boraz the Bold," said Boraz's ghost. "Say it with me. Boraz the—"

"I'm not saying it again!" yelled Jim.

"Some fan you are," said the jilted spirit. "And second of all—*didn't I*?"

Before Jim could get a word in edgewise, he found himself transported back to the Void. Boraz was nowhere to be seen, thankfully, allowing Jim to mutter, "Geez, what a jerk."

"Hey, I heard that!" replied Boraz's disembodied voice.

"Aw, pipe down, Boraz the *Blowhard*!" said a different, much smaller Trollhunter who approached Jim. "You had your chance to teach the rookie. Now it's *my* turn."

"And you are . . . ?" asked Jim hesitantly.

The short Troll stood akimbo and boasted, "I am Merlin's greatest champion! I am he who laughs in the face of danger. I am . . . Unkar!"

"Oh no," said Jim as he felt his body depart the Void once more.

CHAPTER 7
GAGGLETACKED

"I don't like it," Toby said in the Hero's Forge. "Jim's been in there way too long!"

Claire had to agree. Every time she looked at the Soothscryer, its red gem eyes gave her the creeps. It felt like Jim had vanished into the relic hours ago. But when Claire checked her phone, she saw he'd only been gone for less than thirty minutes.

Standing behind Toby and Claire, Blinky and AAARRRGGHH!!! killed time by studying the page depicting Blinky's death. As before, inky drawings of Jim, Toby, Claire, AAARRRGGHH!!!, and Draal all stood in sorrow around their friend's lifeless and crumbled stone body.

"There . . . certainly is a great attention to detail," Blinky said, trying to sound positive.

He forced himself to scrutinize each brutal brushstroke in the hope of uncovering some new bit of information, some potential loophole out of his looming fate. The funeral scene did, indeed, take place in some unfamiliar location. But this time, Blinky noticed something new. His six eyes squinted and saw words written on the crime scene's barren, cinderblock walls.

"That's Trollspeak," Blinky said. "An antiquated Blocking Spell, if I'm not mistaken. But those cinderblocks would appear to indicate a *human* structure. How very bizarre . . ."

"Maybe it's better if you don't keep looking at that page, Blinky," Toby suggested.

"Y-yes, Tobias, perhaps it is," admitted Blinky. "I know it sounds foolish, but I had hoped that *The Book of Ga-Huel* might show some *different* outcome for me this time. But such magical thinking is ludicrous! I . . . I fear I'm losing my mind, my friends."

"No, that's what it *wants* you to think," said Claire flatly. "Us humans have a saying: 'A little knowledge is a dangerous thing.' We don't know the whole story yet, and so *The Book of Ga-Huel* has you questioning yourself. But you can't give in to doubt, Blink."

Stirred, Blinky got to his feet, punched two fists into his other two hands, and declared, "By Gorgus, you're right! Enough of this pointless second-guessing! As soon as Master Jim emerges from that Soothscryer, we shall all unite arm-in-arm, take up the flags of unyielding hope and optimism and—"

"Halt, by the order of the queen!" shouted one of the many Krubera soldiers now rushing into the Hero's Forge.

"—and I'm deader than Disco," Blinky finished miserably.

"Go!" AAARRRGGHH!!! roared at Toby and Claire.

"What about you two?" ask Toby.

"We Trolls will be fine," said Blinky, urgently blocking the Kruberas' view of Toby and Claire with his body. "But you will not. Now heed AAARRRGGHH!!!'s advice and go!"

Toby looked down, seeing a shadow portal open beneath his and Claire's feet. Both teens fell into it and disappeared, just as Queen Usurna stormed into the Forge.

Claire and Toby shadow-jumped back into Strickler's office. Late afternoon sunlight slanted through the windows, and the halls outside had long since cleared of students.

"This place again?" Toby whined. "What's the matter, Claire? One near-death experience at school today isn't enough for you?"

"Hilarious. You and NotEnrique should go on tour together," quipped Claire.

She went back to Strickler's desk and started checking under tidy stacks of paper and inside the drawers. As Claire searched, she said, "This's where we found *The Book of Ga-Huel* in the first place. Maybe there's another clue here to help us save Blinky."

"Good thinking. Don't forget Strickler's secret room behind the bookcase," said Toby.

Claire rifled through school supplies and said, "Yeah, but to open that, we'd need a Changeling Key. And a Changeling to use it. . . ."

"Ugh. On second thought, never mind," Toby said sourly.

He pulled out what looked like a metal

horseshoe from his backpack and added, "I've had enough of Changelings after that close call at the Janus Order. If any of those shape-shifters tries to get the drop on us again, I'll zap 'em with this Gaggletack and expose their true form!"

"Aren't you being a little paranoid?" Claire asked, shutting the last drawer.

Toby opened his mouth to answer, but jumped in place when a different, much louder voice echoed through the school. Claire said, "Was that Señor Uhl?"

Toby cocked his ear toward the hallway and heard what he guessed was a long string of German expletives.

"Um, *sí*," Toby confirmed.

They cracked open Strickler's door and peered down the hall. Uhl's shadow paced in front of his frosted glass windowpane. Toby and Claire traded a nervous look, then tiptoed over.

". . . they will pay," Uhl's invisible guest said. "Tomorrow, the return shall be complete."

Claire and Toby looked at each other again, then at the Gaggletack still clutched like a talisman in Toby's hand.

"By 'they,' do they mean us? And by 'return,' do they mean *Gunmar*?" Toby whispered.

"Are you saying Uhl's a Changeling?" Claire whispered back.

Toby pointed back toward Strickler's office and whisper-shouted, "He wouldn't be the first teacher here that's actually a Troll spy in disguise!"

"This is big," said Claire, trying to process it all. "We need to tell Jim and the others."

Toby nodded in emphatic agreement, and they started edging away from Uhl's classroom—only to back into someone standing right behind them. Shrieking in surprise, Claire cocked her fists, while Toby dropped the Gaggletack onto his toe.

"I'm new here!" said Ellie Stemhower in a rush, holding a clipboard in front of her face.

Claire's sighed in relief at the sight of Ellie. Beside them, Toby hopped on one foot. He gave Ellie the same goofy, love-struck smile despite the throbbing pain in his toe.

"Ellie! What're you doing here?" asked Claire.

"Processing a serious backlog of student late fees," Ellie said, consulting her clipboard. "Do either of you know an Elijah Leslie Pepperjack? That kid's checked out every single book on Mythology, Cryptozoology, and the Solar System! Plus one on coping with bullies and—ooh, what's that?"

Ellie knelt and picked up the Gaggletack. The horseshoe felt heavy, smooth, and cool against the flesh of her right hand as she gave it back to Toby.

"Um, would you believe it's a very big good luck charm?" asked Toby.

"Try telling that to your toe," Ellie snorted.

Toby burst into laughter—like, way too much laughter—prompting Claire to shake her head. Ellie said, "Well, back to the card catalogues. If you don't see me in a few days, call the National Guard!"

"Heh, 'National Guard,'" Toby repeated, admiring Ellie as she walked away. "What a fun sense of humor. And stylish, too! Did you see that red nail polish?"

"No," said a thickly accented voice.

Toby and Claire turned slowly and discovered Señor Uhl seething in the open doorway to his empty classroom. He reached behind his back and said, "What I see are two students in violation of our school's 'no after-hours trespassing' policy. And the price for that is . . ."

Toby and Claire hugged each other and shut their eyes, too terrified to see what lethal Changeling torture device Uhl was about to inflict upon them. But when their teacher brought forward his hand again, it merely held two yellow slips of paper.

"Detention," finished Señor Uhl with a sadistic smile.

CHAPTER 8
HOW UNFORTUNATE

Jim dangled from the edge of the bassinet in the Darklands again. His Eclipse-armored fingers slipped against the chains. And his parched throat could only produce strangled little pleas even though he very much wanted to shout for help at the moment.

The panicked Trollhunter pulled himself fully onto the bassinet, his biceps burning. He tried to catch his breath. Delirious, Jim's vision swam in and out of focus, when something bright flickered at him. It was a golden rectangle bolted onto the other end of the bassinet. Drawn to its glow, Jim leaned closer.

Then he felt the bassinet chains snap, and Jim Lake Jr. plunged into infinite darkness.

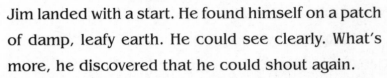

Jim landed with a start. He found himself on a patch of damp, leafy earth. He could see clearly. What's more, he discovered that he could shout again.

"Aaaaah!" cried Jim as he scrambled to his feet.

In addition to the change of scenery, the Trollhunter also noticed that he was back in his Daylight Armor, not the Eclipse version. He mopped sweat off his brow, although Jim couldn't tell if it came from fright or from the increased humidity in this new place—wherever it was. Jim saw a dense canopy of trees overhead, which blocked out the last of the setting sun.

"Had yourself a nightmare, did you?" said Unkar's spirit, which now stood beside Jim. "Waking dreams are sometimes a side effect of these Void Visitations."

Jim heard rustling in the treetops and the faraway caws of tropical birds before asking, "Where did you take me?"

"Not *where*, human Trollhunter, but *when*!" corrected Unkar, who then paused, appearing momentarily confused. "Actually, I guess it's where *and* when. Because we traveled through time and space and—look, kid, we're in the Yucatán Peninsula around 200 CE, okay?"

"Okay, okay," said Jim defensively. "Can I at least ask *why* you brought me here?"

"Oh, for Kilfred's sake! Always with the questions, this one is!" groused Unkar.

The ghostly Trollhunter grabbed Jim's arm and pulled him deeper into the rain forest. They climbed over downed logs and sidestepped snares of roots until they reached a clearing. There, Jim saw a towering stone temple situated in the middle of the jungle. Vines snaked along its steps, and perched golden statues of Mayan gods caught the last of the sinking sun's red light.

Jim then felt a rumble beneath his feet before a gyre burst out of the ground at the base of the temple. The Troll vehicle's circular metal bands slowed to a stop, and Jim now saw that its pilot was none other than Unkar.

"*That's* why," said the ghostly Unkar at his side.

The spying pair moved closer to the Mayan temple, while the living, breathing Unkar exited the gyre. He raised his armored fists into the air and announced, "Behold! Your champion has arrived!

Make way for Unkar the Ultimate!"

Unkar the Ultimate took one step forward, tripped, and fell flat on his face.

"Stop laughing!" Unkar's spirit shouted at Jim, who couldn't help it.

Stifling a few more giggles, Jim then noticed how the rain forest's birds squawked and flew away in a great hurry. Seconds later, a bevy of vine-covered Jungle Trolls descended upon Unkar's prone body. But in one graceful maneuver, the tiny Trollhunter rolled off the ground, formed the Sword of Daylight in his hand, and cleaved through the first wave of enemies.

"Whoa!" Jim gasped.

"Not bad for my first day on the job," agreed Unkar's spirit as he polished his armor.

"Taste the cold, metal sting of my umbrage, you dundering clods!" said the living Unkar to the Jungle Trolls. "You witless louts! You pathetic jackanapes!"

"That's, uh, that's a lot of name-calling there, Unkar," said Jim to his ghost guide.

"Psychological warfare," Unkar's spirit explained. "Softens 'em up before the final blow. Now let's follow him—I—me—myself—*whatever* into the temple!"

71

As the corporeal Unkar hacked his way into the Mayan temple, Jim's mind raced. He had barely been able to wrap his head around the events Boraz the Bold showed him at the Roman Colosseum. And now he was wading through Jungle Trolls in the middle of Central America?

How long have I even been gone? thought Jim. *I've got to get back to the Forge. To my friends. I hope Blinky's okay. That I'm not too late. That he's not already d—*

Jim couldn't bear to finish the idea. His attention returned to the temple, where Unkar the Ultimate had successfully fought his way through an entire army of Jungle Trolls. Bruised and out of breath, the scrappy Trollhunter reached the interior. Torches lit up the enclosed space, which was devoid of any furniture—save for a lone pedestal situated in the middle of the floor. Jim's eyes widened when he saw *The Book of Ga-Huel* resting on top of it.

"But . . . but I don't understand!" Jim stammered. "Why's it here? I thought Gunmar's soldiers took *The Book of Ga-Huel* after they killed Bodus!"

"Gadzooks! Didn't Boraz teach you anything in the Colosseum?" griped Unkar's ghost.

"No!" yelled Jim. "I clearly learned nothing! Nothing at—"

He stopped talking. A sudden thought—a niggling little notion—had been clinging on to the tip of his brain. Jim closed his eyes to better concentrate and connect the dots between what he had seen so far.

"Oh please, human Trollhunter! *Do* go on!" said Unkar's ghost in mock interest.

"I think I've got it," Jim resumed. "Gunmar first wanted *The Book of Ga-Huel* because it might reveal to Orlagk that Gunmar would one day betray him. Spar the Spiteful got in the way—that's why he died. And Bodus must have escaped with the book and come up with the Triumbric Stones—the only way to defeat Gunmar—as a way to protect himself. But Gunmar's soldiers still managed to kill Bodus at the Colosseum and take the book."

"Getting warmer," said Unkar's ghost, while his younger self approached the pedestal.

Jim opened his eyes and said a little less certainly, "And now *The Book of Ga-Huel* is in this temple because . . . because . . . because the humidity is good for the paper?"

Unkar's spirit slapped the back of Jim's head and shouted, "WRONG! See if you can keep up here, kid, will ya? The Jungle Trolls *work* for Gunmar. He gave it to them for safekeeping in this temple, so that no one else would find it. And before you ask, 'Oh, Unkar, why didn't Gunmar just *destroy* the book?' do us all a favor and think about it. If you had a book that revealed a few bad things about you—but that also told the future—would *you* destroy it?"

Jim stopped and considered the question, partly because it was important, and partly because he didn't want to get slapped in the head again.

What would *I do with a book that told the future?* Jim thought. *I'd probably just use it to check on Mom and my friends and make sure they're all gonna be okay. But . . . but if it showed me something terrible was going to happen—like with poor Blinky—what would that mean for the rest of our time together? How could we ever go to the movies or, I don't know, just laugh together, knowing what was waiting for us?*

Jim looked back at his guide with a conflicted frown. Unkar's ghost merely nodded in understanding and once again said, *"That's* why."

They watched the battling Unkar take *The Book of Ga-Huel* and head for the exit.

"So, you got it back? Nice one, Unkar!" said Jim.

"Yeah, the thing about that is . . . ," began Unkar's spirit before loud roars filled the temple.

Jim saw another wave of Jungle Trolls dogpile on top of the real Unkar and drag him to their master— Bular. The sight of Gunmar's vile son made Jim's blood run cold. Even though Bular could not see him—could not hurt him in this Void Visitation— Jim still recoiled in abject terror from the sight of the monster that would nearly kill him one day.

Bular barked orders at the Jungle Trolls, saying, "Toss the Trollhunter into the spike pit so that our Stalkling flock might gorge on his entrails and slurp the marrow from his cracked—"

"Uh, nothing more to see here!" Unkar's ghost hollered at Jim, drowning out the rest of Bular's violent decree. "Nothing at all! And it's, er, probably past your bedtime!"

"No, wait!" cried Jim.

He saw that *The Book of Ga-Huel* had fallen open on the floor. Another dazzling array of light burned from its bindings as a new blank page miraculously started filling with ink.

But Unkar's ghost was in a hurry to leave. He pressed his fingers to both his and Jim's Amulets, which began ticking like two timers. Jim had just enough time to see a blueprint or schematic appear on the lambent page—it looked like an arm, but more cylindrical and segmented—before he and Unkar's spirit returned to the Void.

CHAPTER 9

DEATH BY DETENTION

"So let me get this straight," said Toby. "Señor Uhl punishes us for being at school when it's late—by making us stay at school even *later*?"

"Maybe he is a Changeling after all," Claire deadpanned.

They looked up from their shared table in the school library and out the window. Dusk had already fallen over Arcadia. They were only forty-five minutes into their two-hour-long detention and already bored mindless. At least Claire was.

Toby whiled away the time by stealing glances at Ellie Stemhower. The librarian stamped return dates into books without flourish or fanfare. But to Toby, the menial task took place in slow motion. Each stamp beat in rhythm with his own heart. Ellie's red hair smoldered like fire under the florescent lights. Toby thought he heard romantic music playing in the distance.

"You're drooling again," said Claire.

Toby quickly wiped his mouth with his vest, only to snag the fabric on his braces.

"Owe, gweat," he muttered through a mouthful of sweater.

As Toby tried to disentangle himself, Claire went back to her own private daydream. She thought about Jim, and another pang of worry clenched her stomach. It pained her to leave Trollmarket while he was still in the Void—to leave Blinky and AAARRRGGHH!!! at the mercy of Queen Usurna. But what choice did any of them have? *The Book of Ga-Huel* had brought nothing but uncertainty into their lives ever since they found it. And even if they *did* avert the destiny spelled out for Blinky on that page, what then? As Trollhunters, wouldn't the specter of death always be waiting, ready to strike as soon as they let down their guards?

"Whew!" said Toby, licking his now-freed braces. "That tasted . . . not terrible. I think I'm starting to see why Trolls are into socks."

Claire rolled her eyes before gazing back at her Advanced Placement American History textbook on the desk. All the text started to blur together after nearly an hour's worth of homework. She was about to call it quits for the night, when Claire saw a painting in the book of the signing of the US Constitution. She squinted, leaned closer, and said, "No way . . ."

Toby watched Claire pull out her cell and hold the camera lens over the painting. She pinched her fingers on the screen, zoomed in on the image, then gasped. Toby looked at Claire's cell and saw a close-up of *The Book of Ga-Huel* hidden in the painting. A man with a powdered wig and bright yellow eyes clutched the book, leering behind all the Founding Fathers.

"Are you kidding me?" yelled Toby.

Ellie gave a friendly "Shh!" reminding him to use his library voice. After waving sheepishly at Ellie, Toby softly said, "I've been staring at this painting for *days* in class and never noticed *The Book of Ga-Huel*! Makes you wonder where else it pops up. . . ."

"Yeah," said Claire in a hushed tone. "It does."

She clicked a picture of the painted *Book*

79

of *Ga-Huel*, then opened up her phone's web browser. Toby watched over Claire's shoulder as she then uploaded the photo into the browser's image recognition app. The screen populated with numerous renditions of *The Book of Ga-Huel* taken from other works of art. Claire and Toby's eyes widened. They spotted the timeless tome in a fresco of the burning of Rome, in various Renaissance portraits of yellow-eyed royals, even in a black-and-white photograph of the library aboard the infamous dirigible, the *Hindenburg*. Claire and Toby nearly jumped out of their skin when they heard someone say, *"Gute Nacht."*

Señor Uhl had entered the library and greeted Ellie before shooting a disapproving look at Toby and Claire and disappearing down one of the aisles. Toby stood up with the Gaggletack.

"What're you doing?" hissed Claire.

"Do the math, Claire!" Toby hissed back. "Uhl starts having loud arguments with an invisible someone in his office the *same day* that *The Book of Ga-Huel* turns Strickler's office into a tanning salon! We now have photographic proof that the book was in Germany, which is—oddly—our

Spanish teacher's country of origin! And worst of all, he gave us detention!"

"Well, when you put it that way . . . ," said Claire.

Toby stomped into the aisles and found Uhl in the World Travel section. The stern teacher noticed his student approaching and said, "May I help you, Mister Domzalski?"

"As a matter of fact, yes, Señor Uhl," Toby began politely. "I think we had ourselves a bit of a misunderstanding earlier and—HEY, WHAT'S THAT OVER THERE?!"

He pointed behind Uhl, who turned around to see what the fuss was. Toby rushed forward and pressed the Gaggletack against his teacher's hand. Señor Uhl shrieked and fell backward into the bookshelves. Claire ran up, saw Uhl completely buried under a pile of books, and heard Toby ranting, "Oh my gosh! Oh my gosh! Oh my gosh! UHL'S A CHANGELING!"

Panicking, Claire extended her Shadow Staff and dragged the babbling Toby inside a new portal. The black hole vanished, leaving behind the motionless Uhl—and Ellie Stemhower, hiding meekly behind her clipboard in the next aisle over. . . .

Back in the Hero's Forge, Blinky, AAARRRGGHH!!!, NotEnrique, and Chompsky observed another shadow portal spit out Claire and a blathering Toby.

"Uhl! Gaggle! Book! Tack!" he shouted at his Troll friends.

"Egad! Has Tobias gotten into the Elix-Lore again?" asked Blinky.

"Where's Usurna?" asked Claire, noticing the lack of Kruberas. "Did she take Jim?"

"Master Jim has still not returned from the Void," said Blinky in concern. "As for Queen Usurna, NotEnrique arrived just in time to scare her away with his 'comedy stylings'!"

"Ya should've heard my bit about the Stalkling, the Goblin, and the Helheeti at the beauty pageant," NotEnrique boasted. "It killed!"

"Oh, it *killed* all right—killed any chance we had at convincing Usurna of Master Jim's innocence!" cried Blinky.

Chompsky tilted his Gnome hat at the Soothscryer. Jim stumbled out of a whorl of blue mist and into the Forge. AAARRRGGHH!!! caught him and said, "Had us worried."

"Sorry, big guy," said Jim, getting his bearings. "Blink, turn to page seven hundred and twenty-seven in *The Book of Ga-Huel*!"

Blinky did as told and held up the requested page for all to see. It contained the same blueprint Jim saw in his Void Visitation to the Mayan temple, only now completely rendered.

"Looks like a ruddy arm ta me," NotEnrique said dismissively.

"That's not just any arm," said Jim. "It's a mechanical one. Like—"

"The one I built for Draal," Blinky realized, his six eyebrows cocked in suspicion.

CHAPTER 10
ARMED & DANGEROUS

Draal's metal hand tightened its grip on his ax. The sharpened blade glinted with moonlight as he patrolled the backyard. Casting a look over his spiked shoulder, Draal confirmed the Trollhunter's mother was safe inside her kitchen, still scraping that pan. He then went back to walking the perimeter, keeping watch for any sign of that yellow-eyed figure. Draal saw nothing, but his ears detected a muted *whoosh* behind him. He spun around and found the lights flickering through the basement window—right below Ba-Bru-Ah. Without hesitation, Draal rolled into a ball and launched back into the house via Jim's open window.

Inside the basement, a building shadow portal made the hanging light bulb flicker on and off. Once the vortex grew wide enough, AAARRRGGHH!!! poked his head through—only to get punched square in the jaw by Draal's mechanical arm. Jim, Toby, Blinky, NotEnrique, Chompsky, and Claire all exited the portal in time to see their large friend slam into the floor.

"Draal! What in Gizmodius's name did you do that for?" Blinky demanded.

"He's finally cracked," NotEnrique said. "Was bound to happen, really. Always trainin', livin' alone in a basement, referrin' to himself in the third person—"

"Draal the Deadly has not cracked!" said Draal.

He looked in confusion from his dented hand to AAARRRGGHH!!!, whose eyes and runes now glowed an unusual shade of purple. Blinky rushed over to his best friend and said, "AAARRRGGHH!!!, you must calm yourself! The last time you looked this way, you went berserk after we brought you back to life! This rage you feel is merely a lingering side effect of that dark reanimation spell—don't let it overtake you!"

"You—I—I rushed down here so fast!" Draal stuttered to the furious Krubera in front of him. "I thought you were—"

"TRAITOR!" roared AAARRRGGHH!!! before he decked Draal.

The blow sent Draal flying across the air and smashing into a shelf full of old paint cans. He—and the cans—fell with a loud clatter that echoed all the way to the first floor. Jim heard his mom yelp in surprise and drop the frying pan with a clang.

"Did those dang raccoons get back into the basement?" Barbara asked aloud.

Draal tackled the violet AAARRRGGHH!!! Everyone else gave them a wide berth, not wanting to be steamrolled by their considerable bulk.

"AAARRRGGHH!!! Draal! In Deya's name, stop fighting!" Blinky bellowed.

Pressing himself against the wall, Jim looked up the stairs to the basement door, which Draal had left open in his haste. Barbara's shadow appeared in the hall beyond the doorway, getting closer.

Flinging himself up the steps two at a time, Jim twisted off his Amulet and vanished the armor a fraction of a second before Barbara saw him. He quickly shut the basement door behind him, and blurted, "Mom!"

"Jim?! I thought you weren't home," Barbara said.

"Oh, did you? That's weird! I've been here all the time, uh, pumping iron in the basement," fibbed Jim, before another crash echoed below them. "With, um, Toby."

They heard Toby scream, followed by another loud banging sound.

"Um, that's it, Tobes! Feel the burn!" Jim called down toward the basement.

"Jim, we don't have any weights down there," Barbara said skeptically.

"Right! Right you are, Mom!" Jim stalled. "That's why, instead of weights, we're lifting . . . each other?"

His smile strained to its breaking point. Barbara glanced sidelong at her son and said, "Is that a thing kids are doing now? You know what? Never mind. Just bend with your knees, not your back."

"Fair enough, Mom! See ya!" Jim replied.

He ducked back into the basement, slammed the door shut behind him, and looked down the stairs. Jim's eyes bulged in horror. Draal and the purple AAARRRGGHH!!! still tussled, with Blinky, Toby, Claire, NotEnrique, and even tiny Chompsky trying to pull them apart.

"Jim, hurry!" grunted Claire. "AAARRRGGHH!!! still can't control his temper, and Draal's fighting for his life!"

"Neep, neep!" seconded Chompsky.

"Let go! I've got an idea!" said Jim, leaping off the staircase.

The others distanced themselves as Jim landed on top of AAARRRGGHH!!! and Draal. He wedged himself as far between their gnashing bodies as he could and said, "For the glory of Merlin, Daylight is mine to command!"

As before, a bubble of energy enveloped Jim like a force field. But as it expanded, the bubble pushed apart Draal and AAARRRGGHH!!!, separating them. Now sporting the Daylight Armor, Jim landed between his two stunned friends and said to Claire, "Quick—the woods!"

She channeled another black hole through her Shadow Staff and swept it across every member of Team Trollhunters, herself included. The portal collapsed, the light bulb stopped swinging, and Barbara walked downstairs with a tray of food, saying, "Okay, you buff bodybuilders, Dr. Lake is here with some healthy snacks to boost—"

Barbara dropped the tray on the floor. Not only were Jim and Toby gone, but they had left the basement a shambles, with debris scattered everywhere.

"I'm not cleaning this up!" yelled Barbara as she stomped back up the stairs.

Draal and AAARRRGGHH!!! shook off their lingering dizziness from their impromptu trip to Arcadia's woods and charged at each other again. But Jim stood fast between them, held out his armored hands, and shouted, "STOP!"

The two titans skidded to a halt mere inches from the Trollhunter's body. Draal's chest still heaved from exertion, and AAARRRGGHH!!!'s violet eyes narrowed in disgust.

"This has got to be a misunderstanding," Jim said. "I've known both of you for months, and you've known each other for centuries before that! Everyone just take a deep breath and—"

"Be cool, baby!" Blinky interjected as he, Toby, Claire, NotEnrique, and Chompsky emerged from the woods.

AAARRRGGHH!!! huffed, but then saw the pleading look in Blinky's six eyes. The purple glow on his runes gradually shifted to green before fading altogether, and he reverted to a gentle giant once again. Draal similarly stood down. He lowered his head and said, "Draal the Deadly . . . apologizes."

"Me too," grumbled AAARRRGGHH!!!

"Aw, see? That wasn't so hard, was it?" Toby said cheerfully. "Now, how do you guys bury the hatchet in the Troll world?"

"Why, in cases of a dispute, the two involved parties typically resolve the conflict by bashing their skulls together, until one of them finally passes out," Blinky said matter-of-factly.

"Hmm, why don't we just stick with a fist bump?" asked Toby.

AAARRRGGHH!!! and Draal shrugged, then tapped their stone and metal fists. NotEnrique stared at Draal's prosthetic limb and said, "Oi! Isn't that replacement arm the whole reason this basement brawl started?"

"What're you going on about, imp?" growled Draal, his temper flaring again.

"Easy! Easy!" said Jim. "Draal, there's a *lot* to catch you up on, but we found a drawing that looks just like your mechanical arm in *The Book of*

Ga-Huel. Do you have any idea why it would be in there? Blinky's life could be on the line."

"No, I do not, Trollhunter. I swear it," Draal said, his regret apparent.

"I suppose it is possible I could've fleetingly seen that image during my first reading of the book months ago in Strickler's office," admitted Blinky. "Perhaps it subconsciously influenced me to build a similar prosthesis when Draal was in need of a new arm."

"I wouldn't know anything about that," Draal muttered. "But it stinks of trickery, as does whoever's been spying on the Trollhunter's mother."

"Wait, *my* mom?" Jim asked.

"I have reason to believe that someone has been following Ba-Bru-Uh," Draal said. "I had been tracking him—or her, or it—when your sudden arrival caught me unawares. I thought I had found the culprit and lashed out blindly and . . . well, you know the rest."

Claire covered her mouth and looked at Jim, who seemed stricken by the news. She held his hand and said, "But why would anyone be after Dr. Lake? Any of our enemies who knew she's Jim's mom are either dead or banned from Arcadia."

"I have to get back to her," declared Jim. "Right now. She's all alone."

"I'll go," said Draal, hoisting his ax over his shoulder. "I am duty-bound to protect her."

He gave a curt nod, tucked into a spiked ball, and rolled out of the woods toward Jim's house. Claire gave Jim's hand a squeeze and said, "Don't worry. She'll be safe with Draal."

"I . . . I know," replied Jim. "But now I feel like we're back to square one with *The Book of Ga-Huel*. And if we don't hurry, Blinky could—"

"Could get very sick of seeing all these sad faces!" interrupted Blinky. "With all due respect, Master Jim, I don't know if this day will be my last. But if it is, I certainly don't want to spend it moping around some moonlit forest like . . . like . . ."

"Like a Stalkling, a Goblin, and a Helheeti at a beauty pageant?" offered NotEnrique.

Chompsky squeaked so hard with laughter, he cried. The Gnome removed his hat and used it to dab away his tears.

"I suppose that'll have to do," Blinky murmured in annoyance.

"It doesn't have to," said Toby. "I'm not saying it *is* your last day on Earth, Blinky. But if it *was*, where would you want to spend it?"

Blinky tapped a finger against his pursed lips, deep in thought, before a smile spread across his face. He beamed at his friends and said, "You know, I have *just* the place. . . ."

CHAPTER 11
BURYING BULAR

"What *is* this place?" demanded Gunmar the Black.

The mammoth Gumm-Gumm swiveled his one remaining eye around a showroom decorated with contemporary, yet affordable, human furniture. He kicked over a stand filled with blue and yellow brochures and roared, "This hovel is the vaunted lair of the Janus Order?"

Otto Scaarbach removed his fedora and kneeled before Gunmar. He folded his hands together and begged, "N-no! This is merely a Changeling safe house, great Gunmar!"

"You will address our king as Dark Underlord!" spat Dictatious, his six blinded eyes narrowed in disgust at the sniveling Scaarbach.

"M-my apologies, Dark Underlord," said Scaarbach,

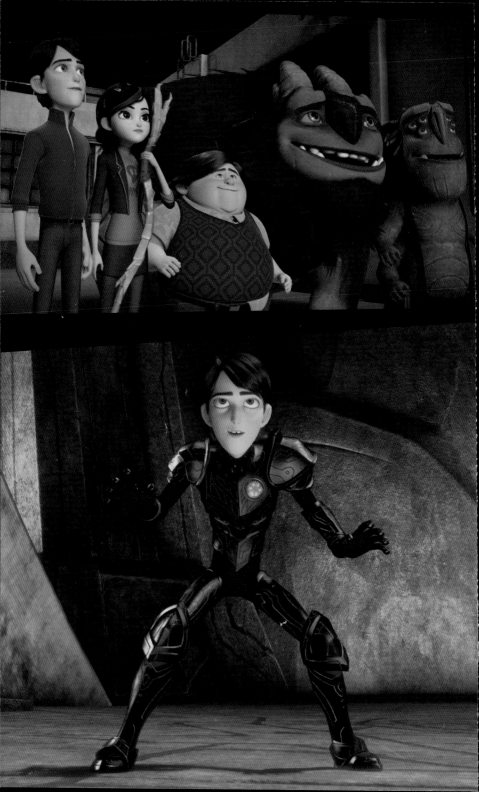

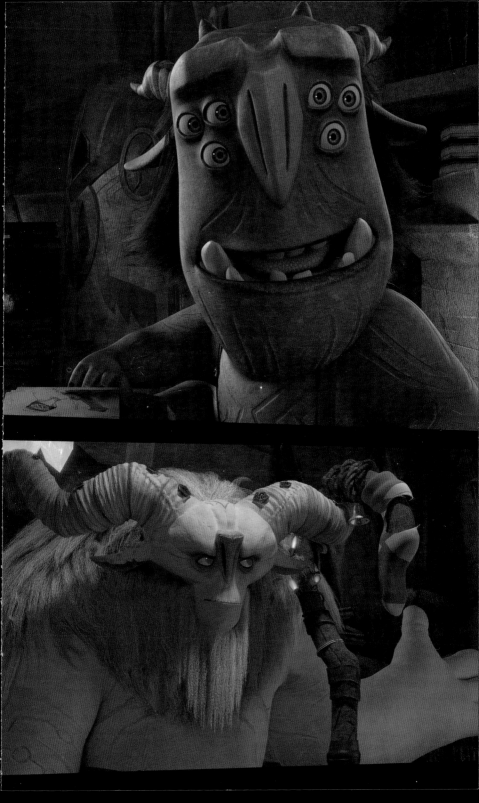

drenched with flop sweat. "But our main base of operations rests beneath the very heart of Arcadia. Preparations are still being made for your glorious arrival, and it will take us at least another night's travel to reach it from these outskirts. I thought it prudent for us to stop here, so that you could . . . rest."

"Rest?" said Gunmar. "Why should I—Gunmar the Black, the Vicious, the Skullcrusher, the Warbringer—ever need rest?"

Even as he said it, Gunmar saw the pale glow in his veins start to fade. It had been so long since he had replenished his power with a true Heartstone. The paltry ergs of energy upon which he subsisted during his exile were unsatisfying at best. And following that accursed human Trollhunter out of the Darklands had taken its toll on Gunmar's reserves, though the defiant Gumm-Gumm would never show even the slightest sign of weakness. In the blink of an eye, Gunmar willed the Decimaar Blade to take shape in his claw. He held the sword's edge up to Scaarbach's twitching face, its unnatural sheen reflecting across the spymaster's glasses. With a dry swallow, Scaarbach mustered enough courage to say, "Th-there is one other reason for this d-detour, Dark Underlord."

"My eyes have failed me, sire, but my ears do detect a twinge of desperation," Dictatious said, stifling another grin. "Could it be that he's *lying* to forestall your righteous judgment?"

"I'd never misdirect you, Gunmar!" swore Scaarbach. "I have devoted my entire existence to your triumph over all the realms—to the Eternal Night you are fated to fulfill!"

Gunmar considered Scaarbach's pledge, then lowered his sword a fraction of an inch and said, "Choose your next words carefully, Impure, for they may be the last you ever utter."

Scaarbach steadied himself with a deep breath and said, "Th-this warehouse holds more than human furnishings. It is also where the Janus Order has been keeping Bular."

Gunmar's single eye widened in uncharacteristic surprise, and Dictatious inhaled sharply. With renewed vigor, Gunmar the Black stood to his full, terrifying height and said, "Take me to my son."

A forklift pulled a large wooden crate from one of the back warehouse's many rows of shelves and lowered it to the concrete floor. Two black-masked

Janus Order agents pried open the crate's lid with crowbars, then backed away reverentially. The warehouse fell absolutely silent, save for the faint whir of the spinning yellow light at the front of the forklift.

Gunmar walked up to the crate, squared his jaw, and looked inside. The broken, rocky remains of his son, Bular, sat in a heap at the bottom.

"We . . . we recovered as much of him as we could from the canal," Scaarbach said from a safe distance. "A torrential downpour made the currents quite strong that day, so there is a slight chance we missed a piece or—"

"Begone," said Gunmar, his back turned, his eyes riveted to the crate's contents.

Scaarbach, Dictatious, and the Janus Order agents were all too happy to leave the warehouse for the front showroom. Once he heard the last of their footsteps fade away, Gunmar the Black reached into the crate. His claw sifted through what was left of his son like so much gravel. The Gumm-Gumm king's entire body shuddered. He retracted his claw and gripped the crate's edge to steady himself. And for the first time in his long, sinister life, Gunmar the Black—the Vicious, the Skullcrusher, the Warbringer—showed weakness.

He threw back his horned head as if he were about to unleash a primal howl. But no sound came. His pitted teeth merely clicked together in a muted wail of anguish and loss.

The forklift's yellow light continued to spin until Gunmar's claw snatched it. He squeezed with all his might, grinding the glass bulb and shell into glittery dust. Gunmar then dropped to his knees, knocking over the crate as he went. Chunks of Bular spilled across the scuffed concrete. When Gunmar opened his eye again, he saw a fragment of his son's face staring back at him from the floor. The Dark Underlord took it in his claws, studying the ossified horn, eye, and bit of upper jaw on the rubble.

"My brutal boy," whispered Gunmar. "My dark prince."

He stood again, righted the crate, and delicately returned the shard of his son's skull.

"Of all my unholy progeny, your appetite for carnage was the most voracious . . . the most like my own."

The glow in Gunmar's veins returned, burning brighter than they had in millennia. He turned his head in the direction of the show room and barked, "Attend me."

Scaarbach, Dictatious, and the masked Changelings scurried back into the warehouse.

"You say the Trollhunter lives nearby? In this *Arr-Cay-Dee-Uh*?" said Gunmar.

"*Ja, mein* Dark Underlord," said Scaarbach.

"Then we must finish the rest of our trek there tonight," decided Gunmar. "I will brook no further delays. Now is the time that I visit my revenge upon Merlin's creation. He may have cut down my son in his murderous prime, but I shall see to it that the Trollhunter suffers before I seal *his* remains in a box."

"As you wish, my liege," said Scaarbach. "And may it please you to know the Janus Order already undermines your nemesis and his allies as we speak . . . with *The Book of Ga-Huel*."

"It still exists?" Dictatious asked in disbelief.

"Quite," Scaarbach bragged. "Better still, one of our top agents has devised a way to author *new* chapters even after Bodus's death."

Gunmar twisted his jaws into an awful approximation of a smile and said, "I would read these chapters, and perhaps write a few of my own—with the Trollhunter's blood for ink."

CHAPTER 12
BACKSTABBER

Blinky had wanted to see day break over Arcadia ever since he beheld his first sunset during the Troll's brief, magical stint as a human.

"Great Gronka Morka," said Blinky in awe. "Is it possible the sunrise is even *more* impressive than its descent?"

It would have been hard for the rest of Team Trollhunters to argue, had they been so inclined. The sun painted vibrant hues of orange and red across the suburbs their bluff overlooked. Normally, this daylight would have proved fatal to Blinky and AAARRRGGHH!!! But Claire had them covered—literally—with an artificial shadow cast by her staff. She turned and smiled at Jim, who sat next to her, typing into his phone.

"Jim, you're missing the best part," Claire said.

"Sorry, just texting my mom," said Jim distractedly. "She seemed pretty miffed about the basement. But now it sounds like it's clean again?"

"Gotta love that Draal," said Toby, putting his hands behind his head and reclining along their grassy lookout point. "He slices, he dices, he does windows!"

"Har, har, Tobes," said Jim, pressing send. "By the way, if she asks, we had a sleepover at your place after our 'workout' last night."

"Neep, neep," said Chompsky of the beautiful sunrise before them.

"Eh, I've seen better," NotEnrique replied with a dismissive wave.

"Well, it's certainly the most radiant sight my eyes have beheld," said Blinky.

"AAARRRGGHH!!! make sure you see another," promised the gentle giant beside him.

Jim looked up from his cell and absently nodded in agreement. But on the inside, he felt slightly less confident about Blinky's chances. Twice now, the Trollhunter had seen *The Book of Ga-Huel* outwit and outlast the Trolls in his Void Visitations, as if the tome willed their deaths—as if it had a cold, calculating mind of its own. Jim struggled with the feeling that he was still missing some big, important detail about the book. Like this blank spot was right in front of the Trollhunter, staring him in the face, and yet he could not see it. And the more Jim tried to focus on the problem, the further it retreated into the murky limits of his understanding.

The whole thing made Jim feel very tired all of a sudden. At least he wouldn't have to worry about his mom for a few hours. Barbara's latest text told Jim that she was about to see patients at the hospital, and Jim figured she'd be safe in such a public setting.

"Hard to believe our party was less than two days ago," Claire sighed.

The friends sat in contented quiet with the memory of their melon bashing before the bushes rustled behind them. They saw Draal trudging out to join them on the promontory.

"Draal, we were just talking about you!" said Toby. "Thanks for the cleanup effort!"

Draal did not answer. Jim studied his face, unable to read the Troll's neutral expression. A new wave of worry hit the Trollhunter, even if he didn't quite know why. Jim's voice cracked as he asked, "Draal? What is it? Did my mom get to the hospital okay? Is she safe?"

"She is," said Draal, devoid of emotion. "But you are not."

Without warning, Draal lunged at Jim, swinging his metal arm like a bludgeon. Reacting on pure instinct, Jim dropped his phone and yanked his Amulet out of his pocket.

"For the glory of Merlin, Daylight is mine to command!" shouted the Trollhunter.

The Daylight Armor's left gauntlet adhered to his arm just in time for Jim to activate the shield. The metal-on-metal impact of Draal's hand on Jim's shield sent sparks flying. As the remaining segments of armor snapped together around Jim, the rest of Team Trollhunters leaped into action. Blinky and AAARRRGGHH!!! were careful to stay in Claire's projected shadow as they barred Draal's path.

"Draal, cease this madness at once!" said Blinky. "How could you, the son of Kanjigar the Courageous, turn on your Trollhunter? In all our years, I never took you for a backstabber!"

AAARRRGGHH!!!'s eyes darkened and his runes glowed purple again, prompting Toby to say, "Uh-oh. Looks like we're in for round two. . . ."

But AAARRRGGHH!!!'s aggressive stance faltered when the wind shifted. His sense of smell had been heightened ever since his resurrection, and AAARRRGGHH!!! widened his nostrils to take in a full range of scents. He wrinkled his nose and said, "Not Draal."

"Do you mean to say this Draal is an impostor?" asked Blinky.

Team Trollhunters surrounded "Draal," who cracked an unsettling, mischievous grin.

"That's gotta be a fake. I've never seen Draal smile!" said Claire.

Once again, the metal-armed Troll pounced at Jim, who raised his shield again. But midway through his jump, Draal's appearance instantaneously changed. His body, normally thick with muscle, streamlined into a lithe form. His rack of horns retreated into his skull, which now sprouted black hair, and his skin shifted from blue to silver. When the attacker landed, he was the spitting image of Jim Lake Jr.—Daylight Armor and all.

"Whaaaaaaaaaaaaaaaaaaaaaaaaaaaaaaaaaaaaa?!" gasped Toby.

"It's another Polymorf!" exclaimed Blinky.

"Neep?" asked Chompsky.

"A Changeling that can assume multiple identities!" Blinky told the Gnome.

Jim ducked as the second Jim took a swing at him, then he kicked away his duplicate. The fake Jim rolled into a crouch before ramming into an unsuspecting Claire—and spinning her Shadow Staff into the bluff's overgrown bushes.

With the staff now out of her reach, the shadow that had been shielding Blinky and AAARRRGGHH!!! dissipated. The two sunlight-averse Trolls had no choice but to jump under the shade of a tree that was near to them, but far from the Jims.

NotEnrique helped up Claire, while Toby and Chompsky tried to tell apart the two identical, battling figures. But the task became impossible with their constant circling and slipping out of each other's armored grips.

"This! Is! Very! Disturbing!" said one of the Jims as the other started choking him.

"Don't try to pretend to be me!" said the other

Jim. "I don't know what you've done with Draal or my mom, but I won't let you hurt any more of my friends!"

The Jims fell to the ground and struggled some more, their entwined bodies rolling toward the lookout point's precipice. Having recovered from the Polymorf's sneak attack, Claire rifled through the bushes for her staff, and NotEnrique shouted, "Hey, AAARRRGGHH!!! Use that supersnout of yers ta sniff out the real Trollhunter!"

Still confined to the rapidly narrowing shade of the tree, AAARRRGGHH!!! inhaled deeply, then said, "Can't—two Jims too far away!"

Jim One and Jim Two came to a stop at the very edge of the bluff, teetering over it. They looked at each other in alarm before the ground gave way beneath their combined weight.

"Help!" yelled both Jims as they fell.

"No!" cried Toby.

Fortunately, one Jim sank his shield into the freshly exposed rock, halting his plummet. He looked down at his ankles and saw the other Jim clinging to them, so that they both dangled precariously from the cliff. Toby, Chompsky, and

NotEnrique rushed over to the brink and pulled both Jims back onto terra firma. Now faced with twin Trollhunters glaring angrily at each other, NotEnrique asked, "How're we ever gonna be able to figure out which one's which?"

Toby didn't even hesitate. He slugged the Jim on the left with his Warhammer, sending him soaring across the lookout point. The remaining Jim rushed forward and hugged Toby.

"Gor blimey!" said NotEnrique. "How'd you know that was the pretender?"

"Are you kidding?" said Toby, hugging Jim back. "I've known this guy since preschool. You think I can't tell which Jimbo's the genuine, sandwich-slinging article?"

"Meatball subs for life, buddy," said Jim in gratitude.

They pulled apart and considered the impostor crumpled against the grassy bluff. The being spasmed and lurched upright. It turned its head toward Team Trollhunters at an unnerving angle, revealing a face that was a nightmarish hybrid of Jim and Draal's likenesses.

"Grumbly Gruesomes!" cried Blinky, turning his

six eyes away from the sickening sight.

The creature screamed a shrill, piercing scream that made everyone cover their ears.

"Um, Claire, any luck in finding your staff?" asked Jim.

"I'm trying!" Claire said, peeking through the dense bushes.

"Please do hurry!" called Blinky from under the tree, their shade now a sliver.

"No pressure," added AAARRRGGHH!!!, moving his singed elbow from the sunlight.

The Polymorf lifted its bent body off the ground, its features shifting wildly between human and Troll attributes. Jim, Toby, and Claire watched aghast as the monstrosity altered its appearance one last time, becoming Señor Uhl before their very eyes.

"You three will be serving detention for a *very* long time," said Uhl in his thick accent.

The Spanish teacher then broke into a run and pulled Blinky out from under the tree.

"Gah!" cried the six-eyed Troll as his skin started to smoke in the sun.

AAARRRGGHH!!! swiped at Uhl, but the renegade teacher dragged Blinky out of his reach. Jim shouted,

"Please! Keep Blinky out of the sun! You'll kill him!"

"If you say so," taunted Uhl.

The shape-shifter tossed Blinky into a public trash can, kicked it down the hill, and ran after it. Jim could hear Blinky's retreating voice as he called out, "Master Jim!"

"Found it!" said Claire, pulling her Shadow Staff from the bushes.

She broadcast a new shadow over AAARRRGGHH!!!, who tore off after his abducted friend. The rest of Team Trollhunters joined the chase, and Jim yelled, "Bring back Blinky!"

CHAPTER 13

AGAINST UHL ODDS

"C'mon, Steve!" whined Eli Pepperjack as the bully held him in a headlock. "It's a Saturday! Can't we just live and let live?"

"Yes, it is, and no, I can't, Pepper*joke*," said Steve Palchuk, squeezing a little harder.

He couldn't believe his luck. Normally, Steve hated doing chores for his mom. She had sent him to the pharmacy on Main Street to pick up some protein powder for her stupid new boyfriend. But once Steve saw Eli walking down the sidewalk, he knew he hit the Pepper*jackpot*.

Steve cocked a meaty fist, ready to punch Eli, when Señor Uhl ran past them on top of a trash can like a lumberjack rolling logs. Their Spanish teacher turned his can off of Main Street and disappeared from view.

"That's actually not the weirdest thing I've seen in Arcadia," said Eli.

Several feet below, AAARRRGGHH!!! galloped full bore down Arcadia's sewers, with NotEnrique and Chompsky clinging to his furry back. The Gnome caught a fleeting glimpse of the trash can through an open manhole cover, and NotEnrique said, "Up there! Turn right!"

AAARRRGGHH!!! rounded the corner and charged down another grimy tunnel, pouring on the speed. Holding his hat in place with one hand, Chompsky chittered, "Neep? Neep, neep?"

"I don't know where those three fleshbags went!" answered NotEnrique.

"On your left!" said Jim, beeping a horn.

He rode his Vespa past them, with Toby and Claire clustered behind him on the scooter's seat. Jim stepped on the gas and said, "Found it right where I left it down here! Good thing Angor Rot didn't trash my ride after I, y'know, accidentally destroyed his soul!"

Seeing a public works construction zone dead ahead, Jim floored it and drove the Vespa up a plywood ramp. The scooter launched through a web of yellow caution tape and orange safety cones, landing on a surface street. Uhl rolled on his can a block away, and Jim accelerated. Noticing the broad daylight reflecting off his armor and the staring pedestrians on the sidewalks, he said, "I'm thinking we need a detour before the whole town learns about our extracurricular Trollhunting activities!"

"On it," said Claire.

A new portal opened up in front of Uhl, sending him and the trash can down to the sewer, heading straight toward AAARRRGGHH!!! Uhl skidded to a halt and started rolling the can backward, only to find Jim, Toby, and Claire motoring out of the shadow portal behind him.

"We've got him now!" said Toby.

Uhl morphed back into Draal, curled his spiked body around the trash can, and spun up and over Team Trollhunters along the rounded tunnel ceiling. Jim squeezed the brakes, narrowly avoiding AAARRRGGHH!!! The Polymorf came to a stop behind them, and an extremely dizzy Blinky clambered out of the dented trash can.

"Great Gronka Mor—BLARGH!" he managed to say before puking.

"I guess the sewer's as good a place as any to blow chunks," said Toby.

Jim said, "Okay, Señor Polymorfo. This is the part where you hand back our friend and tell us what you have to do with *The Book of Ga-Huel*."

"Sorry, Trollhunter," replied the Polymorf, its accent returning as it switched back to Uhl. "But I think you *skipped* a chapter."

Uhl reached into Blinky's belt pouch and pulled out a squat crystal fastened to a handle.

"The Horngazel!" said Claire.

The Polymorf drew the crystal in a glowing arc along the sewer wall, then punched it. A Horngazel passage opened, and Uhl tugged the dazed Blinky into the swirl of stones and light. Jim summoned his Glaives and hurled the spinning blades into the passage right before it closed, becoming solid wall again.

"I can use Blinky as an emotional anchor to get a lock on them!" said Claire.

Team Trollhunters dove into another of Claire's portals and instantaneously emerged three blocks away on Delancy Street, where another Horngazel flashed behind Stuart Electronics. Out came Uhl, the unconscious Blinky, and the boomeranging Glaives. Jim caught his throwing blades and sped after them. Draal's horns sprouted from Uhl's head and bucked the Vespa's tires, making it swerve. Jim regained control of the vehicle and said, "Tobes, take the wheel!"

The Trollhunter jumped off the scooter and followed Blinky and the Polymorf down a new Horngazel passageway. A heartbeat later, he came out the other end—which happened to be on the top side of Arcadia's tallest office building. Uhl waved bye-bye with one of Blinky's limp hands from the roof, and Jim plummeted eight stories to his doom. He shut his eyes as the ground raced toward him, only to feel a pair of sturdy arms catch his body. Jim opened his eyes and saw AAARRRGGHH!!!, NotEnrique, and Chompsky under an umbrella of shadow.

"Close one!" said Toby as he pulled up on the Vespa with Claire.

She shadow-jumped their group to the roof, where they caught the tips of Uhl's horns sinking into a new Horngazel passage. Claire didn't miss a beat. Another portal lowered them one level down to the deserted penthouse floor.

"Good thing nobody's putting in overtime this weekend," said Toby.

They heard the crackle of a Horngazel around the corner. Team Trollhunters raced over and saw Uhl slipping away with the out-cold Blinky. But Jim's armored hands grabbed two of Blinky's, and he and the Polymorf played tug-of-war with the six-eyed Troll. With one final heave, Jim pulled Blinky clear, and the Horngazel passage shut.

"Ha! Got him!" said Toby, before Uhl dragged Jim *and* Blinky into yet another passage.

"Hang on!" said Claire, whipping up another shadow.

She took Team Trollhunters to the seventh floor, where Jim tossed Blinky to AAARRRGGHH!!! before he and the Polymorf disappeared again.

Jim broke free on the sixth floor. Everyone cheered, until the Uhl/Draal hybrid rammed AAARRRGGHH!!! into another Horngazel passage, along with Blinky, NotEnrique, and Chompsky.

While Jim and Claire reclaimed them on the fifth floor, the Polymorf hijacked the Vespa—with Toby still on it.

Fourth floor: They got the Vespa, but no Toby.

Also, Chompsky ran to the men's room.

Third floor: Toby escaped. Blinky woke up. The Polymorf kidnapped everyone else.

Second floor: Blinky rescued his teammates, only to fall into the Polymorf's clutches again.

First floor: Jim, Claire, Toby, NotEnrique, and AAARRRGGHH!!! landed in the lobby level, out of breath and punchy. They readied their weapons in anticipation of the final Horngazel passageway . . . but it never came.

"Blinky?" muttered AAARRRGGHH!!!, his big eyes searching the lobby in vain.

A door slammed behind them, causing the frayed team to turn and yell, "Get him!"

But it was just a startled Chompsky at the stairwell door, a toilet paper streamer trailing from the heel of his little Gnome boot. Jim lowered his Sword of Daylight and said, "They can't have gotten far. Claire, can you hone in on Blink—use him as an emotional anchor again?"

Clare hadn't even bothered closing her shadow portal for those last few floors. She stared at it, concentrating on Blinky, then looked back at everyone with wide eyes.

"I . . . I can't feel him," she said. "It's like he's vanished off the face of the Earth. Or . . ."

"Don't say it," Jim interrupted. "Don't even think it. We'll save Blinky . . . somehow."

A Gun Robot ringtone abruptly blared, making everyone jump again. The Trollhunter twisted off his Amulet in annoyance, vanishing the suit of armor so he could reach the cell in his pocket. Jim saw Barbara's picture on the screen next to a video chat icon.

Jim answered it, angling the camera away from his Troll friends, and said, "Mom, you have no idea how glad I am to see your face, but I can't talk now. We're, um, in the middle of a weekend project with, uh, Señor Uhl."

"But, Jim, that isn't possible," Barbara replied. "I'm looking at Señor Uhl right now."

Doctor Barbara Lake panned her camera across a hospital room, where Señor Uhl lay bandaged and sleeping, his skin swollen and purplish. Jim's mom's head poked back into view, and she added, "The school librarian brought him into the ER last night. What's her name?"

"Ellie," Toby cooed dreamily before Claire flicked his ear.

"Oh," said Jim, his mind racing. "I, uh, meant Miss Janeth. Silly me, I get those two teachers confused all the time! Is . . . is Señor Uhl okay?"

"He will be," said Barbara. "Señor Uhl suffers from extreme allergic reactions to metal. He even has to coat his keys in clear nail polish so they don't make contact with his skin."

Toby gave a nervous chuckle, speed-dialed a number on his phone, and said, "Hello, I'd like to send a floral arrangement to Arcadia Oaks Memorial Hospital. The message on the card should read: *Querido Señor Uhl, por favor, no me mates . . .*"

"Did you know Señor Uhl has a long-distance girlfriend?" Barbara asked. "They met in Barcelona when he was finishing his degree in Spanish. Her name's Susannah."

"Aw, Señor Uhl named his truck after her," Claire said. She smiled.

"You sure it isn't the other way around?" Toby muttered while on hold with the florist. "I bet Uhl only started dating Susannah because she reminded him of his truck!"

"Anyway, the good news is Susannah's flying out here to check on him," said Barbara. "She was supposed to arrive a few days ago, but there was some hold-up with her reservation."

All at once, everything about his Spanish teacher's recent spate of bizarre behavior clicked into place in Jim's mind. He figured Señor Uhl and his long-distance girlfriend probably had been video chatting—just like Jim and his mom were now—on the classroom computer. And all those heated exchanges that Jim, Toby, and Claire overheard about timetables and returns were just about Susannah's delayed flight . . . *not* evil Changeling plans.

Jim became vaguely aware that his mom was saying goodbye to him. He forced a smile at her face on the screen and said, "Sure, Mom. Love you, too. Bye."

He ended the video chat. The remaining members of Team Trollhunters stared at one another in the lobby, aware of the one empty space between them.

"Must find Blinky," said AAARRRGGHH!!!

"But Claire can't track him," reminded NotEnrique. "And if the teacher brace-face almost offed ain't the Polymorf, then who is?"

"Let's just check *The Book of Ga-Huel*," suggested Toby, before face-palming himself. "Which is inside Blinky's pouch . . ."

"It is now," said Claire with dawning realization. "But it wasn't always."

She held her phone up to Jim, showing him the black-and-white photo of the *Hindenburg* library. Jim raised his eyebrows in sudden realization and said, "I need to go to the Void."

CHAPTER 14
SECOND-TO-LAST RITES

Jim and Kanjigar's ghost stood at the foot of a European castle, its pointed turrets backlit by a full moon. The stone stronghold reminded Jim of something right out of a fairy tale—except for the mounds of burning books in the bailey at its center. Both Trollhunters past and present watched as soldiers in severe green uniforms dumped more volumes onto the blaze.

"We must be near Berlin, in the 1930s," said Jim.

"Most astute, young Trollhunter," confirmed Kanjigar. "These jackbooted thugs routinely destroyed any literature that contradicted their leader's mad vision for the future. But this tomecide also served a secondary purpose."

Jim and Kanjigar neared the torched texts, the

soldiers oblivious to their presence. Some donned gas masks to avoid breathing smoke as they raked through the cinders.

"They're searching for something," Jim realized.

"*The Final Testament of Bodus*," said Kanjigar. "A separate text written by the same author of *The Book of Ga-Huel* before his death."

"I'm familiar with it, from *my* time," Jim said. "We thought Blinky had gone crazy when he set the Last Rites on fire. But the ashes revealed a secret message Bodus had left. It spelled out how to collect the Triumbric Stones and defeat Gunmar."

"Correct," said Kanjigar. "Although Gunmar had been vanquished to the Darklands by this point, the Janus Order still contracted these misguided humans to find and incinerate Bodus's Last Rites. This, I could not allow."

The spirit nodded his horns to the side, and Jim saw the living Kanjigar steal into the castle through a tunnel dug by his gyre. The soldiers opened fire on the Trollhunter with their machine guns, but he deflected the hail of bullets with the flat of his Sword of Daylight.

Jim stared agog as his predecessor dispatched

the enemies with unparalleled skill. Unlike Boraz's blunt braggadocio or Unkar's uncivil attacks, Kanjigar the Courageous took no delight in combatting others. He fought thoughtfully, efficiently, never hurling needless punches or insults, only swinging his sword when absolutely necessary. To Jim, watching Kanjigar systematically dismantle this army was like watching poetry in motion. Within minutes, the armored Troll had defeated every single soldier.

"Man, they should've called you Kanjigar the Kick-Butt," Jim said.

He thought he saw the briefest of smiles flit across his ghostly guide's face before they followed the corporeal Kanjigar into the castle's once stately library. Red banners emblazoned with the two-faced Janus Order insignia hung on the walls. Many of the bookcases had already been emptied, their former contents now burned to ash. Kanjigar the Courageous slowly walked past the cases that had not yet been ransacked, the Amulet on his chest ticking louder and faster.

"It's like a Geiger counter," Jim said. "I didn't know the Amulet could do that!"

"You've already unlocked a great many abilities in your short tenure, Trollhunter. But Merlin's contraption still holds a few secrets you've yet to discover," said Kanjigar.

Jim returned his attention to the Trollhunter in the library, whose Amulet now ticked incessantly. This Kanjigar paused in front of a shelf and pulled out a dusty old book that had been sandwiched between other unremarkable works. He tore off its false cover, and Jim recognized the actual book that had been exposed underneath.

"*The Last Rites of Bodus*!" Jim exclaimed to Kanjigar's ghost. "You brought it to Trollmarket. . . ."

"Alas, if only I had succeeded in the other half of my mission," said the spirit.

"So sorry, Kanjigar, but you should've visited this library during open hours," taunted someone from behind, whose voice Jim recognized immediately.

He turned around and saw Walter Strickler at the far end of the library, dressed in all black—and tucking *The Book of Ga-Huel* under his long leather coat. Kanjigar the Courageous raced toward the smug Changeling. Strickler opened a hidden door behind a bookcase and said, "*Auf Wiedersehen*, Trollhunter."

Strickler's laughter echoed along the secret passage as he escaped through it, followed doggedly by Kanjigar. The spirit watched in regret as his younger self disappeared behind the bookcase, then said, "As you can now surmise, the Changeling evaded me on this day—and the many days that followed."

Jim felt his anger rise. He understood that there was nothing he could have done to affect the outcome of this past event, but hearing Strickler's arrogant laugh made Jim want to punch something nonetheless. He took a deep, calming breath and said, "I suppose Strickler hightailed it back to America on the *Hindenburg* and locked *The Book of Ga-Huel* in the hidden room in his office. Where it stayed for nearly eighty years."

"Until you and your allies obtained it," added the phantom Kanjigar. "I know not if this encounter aided in your efforts to rescue Blinkous. But my sincerest hope is that you find him, Trollhunter, and then find a way to rid this world of *The Book of Ga-Huel*, once and for all."

"It's hard to say," said Jim as he started drifting back to the Void. "I doubt I'd know any helpful information if I saw it. I'm not even sure what *questions* I should be asking."

Jim took one last look at the disordered library around them. He didn't know what he was going to tell AAARRRGGHH!!!, Claire, and Toby when he got back. This Void Visitation seemed like their last hope of determining the Polymorf's true identity—and finding Blinky—but now Jim was going back empty-handed and—

"Wait!" shouted Jim. "Kanjigar, take us back!"

The ethereal Troll's Amulet flashed, and they returned once more to the library. Kanjigar's ghost asked, "What vexes you, young Trollhunter? There's nothing new to see here. My memory of this library ended at the exact instant my body left through that passageway."

Jim knew Kanjigar was right, of course. Even now, the library around them appeared static, like someone had pressed the pause button on a video of the past. But Jim turned and faced the last thing he saw as they started heading back to the Void—the red Janus Order banners on the wall. His eyes narrowed, and Jim said, "There may not be anything new, but there is something we haven't seen before, Kanjigar. Look."

127

Jim pointed to the farthest banner, and the spirit beside him now perceived a face peeking out from behind it—the pig-jowled face of a Troll wearing crystal spectacles.

"The Dishonorable Bodus," breathed Kanjigar's ghost. "He was here, in this library! He saw everything—yet I did not see him!"

"Don't beat yourself up, Kanjigar," said Jim, walking closer to Bodus's unmoving form. "You were kinda busy fighting an entire castle full of soldiers and chasing after Strickler. But you must've seen Bodus out of the corner of your eye, even for a second, for him to subconsciously register in this memory."

"But if Bodus was—*is*—still alive, then whose remains did Boraz the Bold inter at the Colosseum?" asked Kanjigar's spirit.

"I think that's the question I was looking for," said Jim. "Now let's answer it."

CHAPTER 15
BODY DOUBLE

AAARRRGGHH!!! left Trollmarket for Rome at midday. But by the time his gyre reached the Colosseum ruins, it was already night, thanks to the difference in time zones. The tourists and street performers in chintzy gladiator costumes had long since left the landmark, so AAARRRGGHH!!! was free to lope onto the arena floor. He started digging his huge paws into the spot Jim had mentioned. After a few minutes of excavating, the gentle giant hit pay dirt.

"Bingo," said AAARRRGGHH!!!

"How's my favorite strongman-slash-emotional-anchor doing?" asked Claire as she emerged from a shadow portal behind him.

By way of answer, AAARRRGGHH!!! tossed

the broken, disinterred body of the Dishonorable Bodus onto the ground before Claire's feet. She had never been to Italy before—heck, she'd never been outside of Arcadia, with her mom's busy political career keeping them local. But Claire hoped the next time she was in Europe, it'd be under less morbid circumstances. She nudged the stone remains with the tip of her shoe and said, "Is it him?"

AAARRRGGHH!!! picked up one of the flinty pieces and sniffed it. He stuck out his tongue and shook his head, as if reacting to a pungent scent, then said, "Not Troll. Smell like fake Draal. Smell like Polymorf."

"So Jim was right," Claire said, putting the puzzle pieces together in her mind. "Bodus used a Polymorf body double to fake his death. C'mon, AAARRRGGHH!!! We need to get back to Trollmarket and tell the others."

"C'mon, AAARRRGGHH!!! We need to get back to Trollmarket and tell the others," Claire's voice echoed into the Void.

Jim watched in wonder through one of the afterlife's floating, circular windows as Claire and

AAARRRGGHH!!! returned to the gyre and sped home. He was so engrossed, Jim didn't even notice Deya the Deliverer's translucent spirit manifest behind him. She studied the young Trollhunter for a moment, just as Jim studied his friends, before saying, "You care deeply for them. I can tell from the way you peer through the Void's scrying portal."

"They . . . they're everything to me," said Jim. "All my friends are."

Even NotEnrique, thought Jim to his own astonishment.

Normally, the little Changeling irked Jim. But after he had emerged from Kanjigar's Void Visitation and sent AAARRRGGHH!!! to confirm a hunch at the Colosseum, Jim asked NotEnrique to check on his mom and the real Draal. The Trollhunter half expected the impish Changeling's retort to be some sort of punch line. But NotEnrique surprised Jim— and maybe even himself—when he said, "I'll guard 'em with me life. No joke, Trollhunter."

At a loss for words, Jim had watched NotEnrique and Chompsky dutifully depart for his house before he reentered the Void and found this scrying portal. It was as if this strange realm anticipated what the

Trollhunter wanted before Jim even did.

"Say, Deya, these scrying portals don't show you *everything*, do they?" asked Jim.

Specifically, he was concerned about their ability to spy on him during potentially embarrassing moments. Like when Jim would sing slow jams in the shower, for example.

"Not everything, Trollhunter," Deya replied. "We do value some modicum of privacy."

"Oh good," said Jim, trying to mask his great relief. "I, uh, don't suppose you've had any run-ins with *The Book of Ga-Huel* too?"

"No, I cannot say I ever spied its pernicious pages," Deya replied. "Yet I remain all too familiar with enemies who trade in deception. From Changelings to Polymorfs to Trickster Trolls to Glamour Masks that conceal one's true identity, it has ever been difficult for Trollhunters to tell friend from foe."

"No kidding," said Jim, crestfallen. "I once met this Heetling named Rob, who—Deya?"

Jim became abruptly aware of the fact that Deya's ghost had vanished. He turned around, not seeing her anywhere in the Void, which now appeared much darker. His skin prickled with goose bumps. Jim looked down and saw that he once again wore the Eclipse Armor.

"Oh, no," uttered Jim before the Void evaporated beneath his feet.

As before, Jim fell through the Darklands for what felt like an eternity. His flailing arms reached out and—just as before—snagged a series of coarse hanging chains. The Trollhunter broke his fall and swung like a pendulum over the bottomless black pit.

"This isn't real!" Jim said. "It's another waking dream from the Void Visitations!"

But no matter how hard he tried to convince himself, Jim remained hanging there like bait on a lure. His metal-covered fingers started to slip on the links, and he thought he heard the slither of a nearby Nyarlagroth.

"Or not!" Jim said with rising panic.

Thinking fast, he summoned his twin Glaives—both black and red to match the Eclipse Armor. Gripping one blade in each hand, Jim swung his right arm upward and wedged the Glaive into the open center of link over his head. He pulled himself up and repeated the same motion with his left arm. Bit by bit, link by link, the Trollhunter hoisted himself up the chain until he reached the Darklands' Changeling nursery. He clambered onto the same bassinet from his previous nightmares, more inconsolable baby cries ringing in his ears.

Jim clamped his eyes shut in a feeble attempt to drown out the plaintive wails, but still they came. When he reopened them, Jim saw that gold glint again. It reflected off the small metal plate screwed into the opposite end of the bassinet. The Trollhunter squinted at the gilded rectangle and, this time, he could discern letters on its surface.

Ignoring the baby shrieks and the roars of oncoming Nyarlagroths, Jim pulled himself into the empty bassinet and read the words etched onto the golden name plate.

"Of course!" said Jim, thunderstruck with sudden understanding.

"What's that, Trollhunter?" asked Deya the Deliverer.

Jim startled, then found himself back in his Daylight Armor and in the Void with the fallen Trollhunter's see-through spirit.

"Deya! You're back!" cried Jim. "I'm back!"

"But neither of us ever left," she said, not quite following him.

"I was in the Darklands! Again! I mean, sorta!" babbled Jim, his mind racing.

"Ah," said Deya in dismay. "It would only make sense for you to experience flashbacks from your ordeal in that dismal dimension. I, too, suffered fitful dreams for years after the Battle of Killahead Bridge."

"No, it's not like that," Jim replied, his eyes wide with insight. "At least, not *only* like that. I think the Void wanted me to have a visitation to one of my *own* memories. I think I just solved the mystery of *The Book of Ga-Huel*!"

CHAPTER 16
IF THIS BE MY TOMB

Six bleary eyes fluttered open. Their pupils dilated, trying to focus on an unfamiliar setting. With a groan, Blinky tried to sit up, but found himself bound to an ornately carved stone table.

"A Gumm-Gumm sacrificial altar," Blinky rasped in recognition.

"It dates back to the Mayan empire," said a being outside of Blinky's blurred field of vision. "You might find it interesting to note that your previous protégé, Unkar, also occupied that altar, until Bular—ah, but what kind of author spoils the ending to a story?"

Blinky turned his head and saw a potbellied, bespectacled Troll shuffle into view.

"The Dishonorable Bodus," Blinky sneered.

"Not much as far as pen names go, is it?" replied Bodus. "But I'll take it—and take so much more. Starting with this . . ."

Bodus held out Blinky's Horngazel key and began writing with it along the walls, tracing over some old Trollspeak graffiti on the cinderblocks. The faded words suddenly glowed red, as if refreshed. Blinky shivered, recognizing the writing on the walls from that dreadful page in *The Book of Ga-Huel*.

"That's the only problem with these Blocking Spells—they need to be rewritten every few hours," Bodus said, appraising the crystal key in his hand. "Still, what a curious implement, this Horngazel. It likely draws from the same inexplicable inkwell as my own quill of choice. I'd best jot down this finding in the appendix."

Blinky watched Bodus waddle over to a dim corner of the enclosed space, where *The Book of Ga-Huel* sat open on a desk of human origin. Bodus set down the Horngazel, retrieved his crystal pen, and began drawing with it upon his own protruding belly. Blinky gawked in confusion as he watched the writing disappear from Bodus's belly and then reappear on *The Book of Ga-Huel*'s next blank page. The parchment blazed with blinding light, forcing Blinky to turn away from it. But Bodus's eyes remained unaffected behind his crystal spectacles.

"Then it is you who has been adding pages to that book of late," Blinky said.

"With some help," said a German-inflected voice.

Blinky craned his head and saw the patchwork Polymorf lurking in the cinderblock chamber. Troll horns wreathed Uhl's head like antlers, and a Troll dagger gleamed in his hand. Fluorescent liquid coated the blade, a fat drop beading onto the knife's point.

"Creeper's Sun," said Blinky, recognizing the toxin that once turned AAARRRGGHH!!! to solid, lifeless stone. "If this be my tomb, then get on with it, Polymorf. All I ask is that you spare my friends' lives when they come to grieve over me, as predicted on that profane page!"

"Do you really think you're in a position to make requests?" asked the Polymorf, the accent wavering. "And there's no way your friends will ever find my secret lai—"

The Sword of Daylight thrust between two

cinderblocks an inch from the Polymorf's nose. Using the wide blade like a lever, Jim pried open a hidden door in the wall from the outside.

"Master Jim!" Blinky exclaimed.

The Trollhunter slashed away the ropes tying Blinky to the altar. Toby, Claire, Draal, and AAARRRGGHH!!! barged in after him, the Arcadia Oaks High School library visible behind them. Toby looked at the bookcase disguising the other side of the cinderblock door and said, "Guess Strickler's office wasn't the only room with a hideout built into it. Our school is weird."

"And tagged with Trollish Blocking Spells," added Claire, identifying the words Bodus scrawled along the walls. "No wonder I couldn't 'feel' Blinky with my Shadow Staff."

Draal cornered Bodus, while AAARRRGGHH!!! swallowed up Blinky in a great bear hug. The horned Uhl went red in the face and yelled at the teenagers, "You three delinquents will be expelled from this school—and from life!"

"You can drop the Uhl act now," Jim said to the Polymorf. "I know your *real* identity. Turns out I've known ever since I read it in the Changeling nursery back in the Darklands. Isn't that right . . . Eloise Stemhower?"

The Polymorf's smirk faltered before its entire body shrank and sculpted itself into the petite, redheaded frame of Ellie, the new school librarian. She snorted another adorable laugh and said, "Gosh, guys, you can just call me Ellie. All my students-slash-victims do."

"What do your bosses in the Janus Order call you?" asked Claire, tightening her grip on the Shadow Staff.

"Just because they're Changelings doesn't make 'em my bosses," said Ellie. "I sell my protection, infiltration, and execution services to the highest bidder. And nobody's been more desperate to pay me than ol' Bodus here. We've been thick as thieves ever since I smuggled him outta Berlin. I mean, who could possibly be a better double or triple agent than a Polymorf?"

"I . . . I think I'm gonna be sick," Toby groaned, his cheeks puffing with nausea, then deflating. "How come you didn't get exposed by the Gaggletack? I saw you touch it with your bare hand! Your delicate, porcelain-skinned bare hand . . ."

"What, you mean this hand?" asked Ellie, holding up her dagger-wielding left arm.

The revealed Polymorf then held up her right, which transformed into its true form—a mechanical, prosthetic arm, not unlike Draal's—and said, "Or *this* one?"

"I guess I meant the one without the potential murder weapon, but they're both pretty bad," Toby said, his heart sinking.

"Aw, sorry, kid." Ellie mock pouted. "Gaggletacks don't work on metal, even when it's made to look like flesh. But at least you'll all be dead soon. Starting with your biggest target!"

The rest of Ellie's body reverted to its actual state—that of a reptilian, chalk-white Polymorf Changeling with a false arm—and hurled her poisoned knife at AAARRRGGHH!!!

"No!" cried Blinky.

The six-eyed Troll stood protectively in front of his much larger teammate, shielding AAARRRGGHH!!! with his own body, and prepared for the worst. The dagger closed in on Blinky's heart—before bouncing off Jim's raised shield. The Trollhunter glared at the albino Polymorf and said, "I don't care what that stupid book says. Blinky lives. The end."

"Typical," spat Bodus. "Everyone's a critic!"

The porcine Troll held open the tome at Team Trollhunters, shining its dazzlingly bright light at them. They all ducked behind the altar, but the glare left Toby, Claire, Draal, and AAARRRGGHH!!! groping in the dark.

"Can't see!" grumbled AAARRRGGHH!!!

"Me neither!" said Toby. "Now I know how Nana feels without her glasses!"

Claire blinked a few times and said, "I think it's just temporary! We didn't look directly at it. We just need enough time for our eyes to adjust!"

"Then it is time you shall have!" declared Draal.

He hunched into a tight ball and blindly rolled around the cinderblock chamber. His spiked body missed the Polymorf but bowled over Bodus, knocking *The Book of Ga-Huel* from his hands. Jim watched the piggish Troll scurry into a corner, the bright spots now fading from the Trollhunter's recovering vision. He next saw the Polymorf lunging for Blinky, and pulled his six-eyed friend clear of her metal hand.

"We gotta get you someplace safe!" Jim said to Blinky.

But the Polymorf tackled both of them behind the desk while Bodus, still unseen in the corner, put down his crystal pen and picked up the dagger. AAARRRGGHH!!!, Toby, Claire, and Draal's sight all returned, but they still couldn't see much of the struggle on the other side of the desk.

"Now, Blinky!" shouted Jim.

The six-eyed Troll sprang up from behind the desk and made a break for the library—only to run into the poisoned dagger held by Bodus. His four arms grew rigid. Blinky took one last look at the horrified Team Trollhunters before his body turned to stone and fell apart.

CHAPTER 17
GHOST WRITER

"Spoiler alert, Trollhunter!" cackled Bodus. *"The Book of Ga-Huel* is never wrong!"

Jim rushed out from behind the desk and knelt beside Blinky's fractured husk. Claire, Toby, Draal, and AAARRRGGHH!!! all gathered in mourning around him, tears streaming from human and Troll eyes alike.

"What did he ever do to you?" Jim said bitterly to Bodus.

"Nothing," smirked the bespectacled Troll. "But if one is to destroy a team, it only makes sense to start with its most learned member."

AAARRRGGHH!!! tried to fit Blinky's pieces back together, but they just crumbled to dust in his paws. Toby and Claire hugged his furry back in sympathy, in grief.

"Without the sage guidance of Blinkous Galadrigal, you and your allies with perish in short order," the Dishonorable Bodus continued. "I will use that victory to make up for all the bad things I wrote about Gunmar and reenter his good graces—'good' being a relative term, you understand. Ah, but I digress! My deeds will impress upon Gunmar the need to call off his assassins. I won't need a Polymorf bodyguard ever again! In time, the Gumm-Gumm king will come to see me not as a liability, but as the oracle who shall foresee his violent path to victory!"

"That's never going to happen," vowed Jim, wiping his eyes with his gauntlet. "Gunmar's trapped in the Darklands forever."

Bodus smiled in malevolence and said, "Boy, are you in for a plot twist."

"I could say the same of you," announced a rich, sonorous voice recognized by every surviving member of Team Trollhunters.

Bodus turned toward the desk and found Blinky staring back at him. The Troll crossed his four arms and grinned with the confidence of someone at a superior advantage. Stunned speechless, Bodus looked at the others. Toby, Claire, Draal, and AAARRRGGHH!!!

dropped their sad pretenses, and Jim held aloft the stone Blinky head. The Trollhunter pulled on its face, tugging free an odd, Tiki-like Troll mask.

"A Glamour Mask!" seethed Bodus.

Beneath the mask, he saw the petrified grimace of the Polymorf once named Eloise Stemhower— Ellie, to her students-slash-victims.

"She didn't even realize Jim had placed the Glamour Mask onto her during our struggle," said Blinky. "How's *that* for a plot twist?"

Bodus backed away from Team Trollhunters and stammered, "B-but I saw your faces! Y-you wept for your friend!"

"Acting!" Toby yelled dramatically.

"And we had a good teacher," said Draal.

He clapped his mismatched hands in applause while Claire took a modest bow. Bodus gaped in bewilderment before Blinky shoved him against the cinderblock wall. He cocked his hands into four fists, and Bodus squealed, "You wouldn't hit a Troll with glasses, would you?!"

"Not normally, no," admitted Blinky. "But six eyes are greater than four. So, in your case, I'll make an exception!"

Blinky socked Dishonorable Bodus clear across the face, knocking off his spectacles. He embraced his teammates and said, "Now that the future foretold by *The Book of Ga-Huel* has come to pass— more or less—we needn't run from it anymore, my friends."

"Who doesn't love a happy ending?" Jim said as he fist-bumped Blinky four times over.

"This isn't how it ends!" shrieked Bodus.

Jim and the others returned their attentions to the defeated author. He scrambled across the floor for his crystal pen, then began scribbling furiously on his belly again. The writing disappeared from Bodus's flesh, and he held *The Book of Ga-Huel* in front of his face to see it transcribed across a blank page.

"Forgetting something?" said AAARRRGGHH!!!

He pointed to the pair of cracked spectacles by his large foot before stomping on them. The Dishonorable Bodus's unprotected eyes looked back in horror upon *The Book of Ga-Huel*, and the intense glare of its newest page was the last thing he ever saw. The tome grew too heavy for the brittle hands that held it. Bodus's fingers crumbled, and the book dropped into his still, stone lap, where it stopped shining.

Jim and Blinky braved a look at the latest entry in *The Book of Ga-Huel*. It bore a single image of a potbellied Troll, his porcine face frozen in a scream, an open book resting in his still, stone lap.

LEFT OF TODAY

After the Saturday sun set over Arcadia, Blinky requested that Team Trollhunters gather in Jim's backyard. Jim, Toby, Claire, AAARRRGGHH!!!, Draal, NotEnrique, and Chompsky all sat in silence on the lawn as their six-eyed friend stood before them. At first, Blinky couldn't seem to find the right words. He seemed rattled by his near-death experience.

"C'mon, Blink, you can do it," Jim encouraged.

Blinky closed his eyes, took a deep breath, and said, "The events of this past week have taught me a lot about life. About how fragile and precious our existence truly is."

The teammates all looked at one another, moved by Blinky's sentiments. Jim and Claire held hands. Toby cozied up beside his Wingman. And Chompsky tried to hug NotEnrique, who initially balked—only to roll his eyes and hug the little Gnome back.

"Although some might argue that each sunrise and sunset only brings us closer to our inevitable demise, I now see that each day is a new opportunity as well," Blinky continued. "A chance to be with those we love and to appreciate the very privilege of drawing in breath for even one more hour, minute, or second. And so, my friends, I can think of no better way for us to celebrate life together . . . than to mindlessly detonate melons with miniature novelty explosives!"

Everyone cheered as Blinky rolled out an enormous watermelon and lit the fuse poking from its rind. AAARRRGGHH!!! leaned closer to Blinky and whispered, "What's in it?"

"Dwärkstone grenades," Blinky whispered back.

"Three! Two! One!" the group counted down.

The melon hit critical mass, exploding like a supernova star, and Team Trollhunters frolicked in the shower of juice and seeds. Jim felt his cell buzz in his back pocket and saw a text message from his mom on its screen.

R U ok? Just heard a really loud bang all the way

at the hospital, read Barbara's text.

Bang? What bang? Jim texted back, while Blinky lit another fuse. All good in the neighborhood, Mom.

Glad to hear it, read Barbara's response. Love U.

Love u 2, Jim texted back before getting drenched by another melon wave.

Claire almost slipped in a juice puddle while walking over to him. She combed some pulp out of Jim's hair, saw his smile, and said, "You look relieved."

"I am," Jim admitted. "I mean, I guess I need to make peace with the fact that I'm always gonna worry a little about the people I love. But Blinky's alive, my mom's safe, and the Polymorf that was stalking her is history. So I'm gonna try to enjoy what's left of today and deal with tomorrow . . . well, *tomorrow*."

"Wow. Very mature, Lake. Almost makes up for you drooling after the evil school librarian," Claire said, imitating Ellie's snort.

"C'mon, Nuñez, I said I was sorry," said Jim with a laugh. "And she wasn't even my type. Seriously! I like girls who . . . who are fearless. And into Papa Skull. With blue streaks in their hair. And who wield arcane shadow powers through a haunted staff they stole from a soulless Troll killer. Y'know, typical teenage girl stuff."

Claire self-consciously tucked her blue streak behind her ear and said, "Wow. Hearing the way you describe your type, she sounds kinda . . ."

"Awesome," Jim said. "She kinda is."

Jim leaned his face closer to Claire's, their lips almost touching, when—

"Hey, did anyone else have bits of melon land where the sun don't shine?" yelled Toby.

Claire and Jim cringed as Toby walked awkwardly past them, his body making disturbing squishing sounds with each step. Toby stopped midsquish, saw Jim and Claire glaring at him, and said, "Oh. Uh, sorry?"

"Well, if *that* didn't kill everyone's appetite, I'm firing up the grill," announced Jim. "Who's hungry?"

"Neep!" said Chompsky.

"As is Draal the Deadly," added Draal.

"Who still speaks in the third person . . . ," muttered NotEnrique.

Jim arranged a pyramid of charcoal briquettes inside his barbecue, squirted them with lighter fluid, and lit the entire thing with a match. Flames grew and crackled, but Jim knew he'd need a little more kindling to get the right level of heat for grilling.

The Trollhunter took one last look at *The Book of Ga-Huel* before tossing it into the barbecue. Jim had already seen one book burning too many in his life, but he knew this tome was simply too dangerous to be left out in the world, unguarded and unchecked. The leather cover started to blacken and curl, and only now did Jim begin to feel the warmth coming from the grill. He closed the lid, turned his back to the book, and rejoined his friends.

"What's this thing with the melons?" complained Unkar the Unfortunate.

"I deem it a fitting tribute for the young Trollhunter who reveres me so," boasted Boraz the Bold. "Why, it reminds me of the many feasts prepared in my honor during Trollkind's greatest holiday—Boraz the Bold Day."

Kanjigar the Courageous and Deya the Deliverer ignored Boraz's haughty laughter and went back to looking at Jim through their scrying portal in the Void. Their vigilant spirits watched as he and his friends went into Jim's kitchen and raided the fridge for food to grill.

"The human grows in skill," said Deya.

"Indeed," Kanjigar replied. "Out of our entire host of Trollhunters, only he proved capable enough to solve the longstanding mystery of *The Book of Ga-Huel.*"

"I had my doubts about his worthiness to wear Merlin's Amulet, but they have long since passed," Deya said. "My only hope is that he does not carry with him the burdens that plague all Trollhunters, for they are legion."

Kanjigar gestured into the mist. The scrying portal fast-forwarded a few hours and provided them with a lens into Jim's bedroom. The ghostly Trollhunters watched Jim sleep peacefully, while Barbara sat in her scrubs on the corner of the bed, having just returned from work. She kissed her son lightly on the forehead and whispered, "Sweet dreams, kiddo."

"No nightmares trouble him this evening, which bodes well," said Kanjigar's spirit. "Jim Lake Jr. has successfully fought the future, but needs rest before confronting his next challenges in the *past*."

The scrying portal view shifted. It pulled outside of Jim's bedroom window and looked down at the backyard, where a pair of yellow eyes shone in the night. They belonged to a lurking figure—the very same who had spied on Barbara nights ago. The figure stepped out of the dark, and Walter Strickler stood revealed in the moonlight.

The Changeling watched the light in Barbara's bedroom window go out, then reached into his tweed sports coat. Strickler pulled out the charred, but still intact, *Book of Ga-Huel*. He had retrieved it from the flames earlier, when the Trollhunter and his allies went into the kitchen, then kept his distance until they left for good.

A stiff wind whistled across the yard, blowing open the book to one of its earliest pages. Strickler's eyes flared yellow as they took in the overlooked chapter. It featured an old drawing of Jim in his armor, fighting for his life in the middle of an epic Gumm-Gumm war. The date inked below it read 501 CE.

"What have you gotten yourself into this time, young Atlas?" said Strickler with a sly grin. "It would seem I've returned in the proverbial nick of time.

Clearly, my former pupil will soon need *additional* training. And who better to give it than his favorite teacher?"

With a cruel laugh, Walter Strickler closed *The Book of Ga-Huel*, and Jim Lake Jr. felt the onset of a whole new nightmare.

RICHARD ASHLEY HAMILTON

is best known for his storytelling across DreamWorks Animation's How to Train Your Dragon franchise, having written for the Emmy-nominated *DreamWorks Dragons: Race to the Edge* on Netflix and the official DreamWorks Dragons expanded universe bible. In his heart, Richard remains a lifelong comic book fan and has written and developed numerous titles, including *Trollhunters: The Secret History of Trollkind* (with Marc Guggenheim) for Dark Horse Comics and his original series *Scoop* for Insight Editions. Richard lives in Silver Lake, California, with his wife and their two sons.